Return To Gray Harbor

J.J. Bryant

Steven —
Thank you for
being a wonderful & supportive
friend! I hope you enjoy my
book!
Best,
JJ

JJ Books
est. 2015

www.jjbookspress.com * Somerville, MA

JJ Books are published by J.J.I Productions, LLC.

Somerville, MA

Cover Design by M. Weiskind

Cover Image: Shutterstock

Edited by J.Imbriani and ebookeditingpro

First published as an ebook May 2015 and as print on demand: July 2015

ISBN-13: 978-0692445082
ISBN-10: 0692445080

DEDICATION

To my family new, old and chosen – you can always
change course and always return to those that matter
and start over. This book is for all of you. Thank you
for believing.

CONTENTS

ACKNOWLEDGMENTS

Big thanks to Lisa, Laura, Jessica, Noel, Beth, Dana Blu, Carissa, Alan, Brian, Chris, Miriam and Penny who all inspired and supported me. And a big thanks to the rest of my family. This book would never have happened without your patience, advice, love and coffee!

PROLOGUE

"What do you mean, you're moving to New York?"

Though James Malone said the words in a quiet tone, eighteen-year-old Michael Malone knew better.

He was in big trouble.

What else was new? He always disappointed them because he could never live up to the memory of his football star brother. Michael had dreams, dreams that didn't involve gutting fish his whole life or living in Maine under the shadow of his brother's tragedy.

Michael relaxed his shoulders and took a deep breath, then began to state his case.

"They've offered me a full scholarship. It's one of the best schools in the country."

What he left out was that he intended to study Corporate Finance. He also didn't mention that in addition to NYU, he had applied to half a dozen other schools even farther away from Gray Harbor, Maine. He just had to get away from his hometown. And more importantly, he had to get away from Malone's Market,

1

his father's prized business.

His father was always a tough one. He always got his way. Everyone followed his lead. And if you didn't, you had to be prepared to hear it: a long winded lecture that started quietly and ended like a shipwrecked boat. It wasn't going to be that way this time. Michael was always the quiet one, but not anymore — things were going to change.

Before his brother Jesse died, Michael's father had talked about how once Jesse and Michael both finished college the store would become Malone and Sons' Fish Market. They would study business like he did and together, they would make Malone's more than a fish market, but a destination in Maine. James felt that someday everything on Penobscot Bay, especially Gray Harbor, would become a tourist destination.

He always said, "anything by the water, especially in Maine, is gonna be a money-maker someday. After all, this is 'Vacationland,' so of course someday people will come to Gray Harbor, and when they do we'll cash in."

Michael's thoughts were interrupted by his father's voice, which had risen slightly. "You already have a scholarship."

"The University of Maine is a damn good school. Your grandfather went there, I went there, your brother Jesse was going to go there ... and YOU are going to go there!"

The quiet voice had turned to rage. His dad started to shuffle things around on the dining room table as if the conversation were over, case closed. The great James Malone had spoken.

Michael just couldn't take it, he pushed his slightly

too-long brown hair out of his eyes, adjusted his thick horn-rimmed glasses, and said, "Well, Dad, maybe it's just not good enough for me." He tried to say it with confidence, though he looked anywhere but into his father's eyes. "I'm moving to New York. School starts in August."

"Oh, Michael, think about this," said his mother, Marty, sounding disappointed as she walked into the room. Michael let out a sigh. That's just what he did, he disappointed everyone, he thought to himself.

"He doesn't need to think about this, he's not going. He has a responsibility to this family."

"It's too late, Dad..." Michael said, and lifted up his head defiantly.

James straightened and dropped the mail he had been sifting through onto the dining room table, which he frequently used as his office, and leaned forward. "You accepted and decided to move four hundred miles away without even talking to us first?" James was almost yelling now. He had always had a temper. Whenever he got angry, what appeared to be a large vein throbbed on the forehead of his handsome face and he turned red.

In his most mature sounding voice, Michael said, "I'm eighteen, and I don't need permission." He swallowed but the lump in his throat just wouldn't go away.

"Annie got married when she was only twenty and no one batted an eye..."

"You are my son, not Annie, and that is different," said James in an exasperated tone.

Annie had married her soldier boyfriend, Tom Mendelson, before he shipped off for a tour overseas.

Everyone in the family loved Tom. The Mendelsons were a good family and came from a long line of soldiers and lobstermen. Annie was finishing up school at a local commuter college and planned to work for Malone's Market full-time when she was done. Even though she had gone and married young against her parents' wishes, she was still falling in line in her own way by staying local and working for the family business.

"That's the problem, isn't it, Dad? I'm not Annie and I am certainly not Jesse, right?"

"That's enough, Michael!" his mother exclaimed, her voice shaking. "We don't compare you to anyone, you are just you. We would never even try to compare you to your brother or sisters."

Michael raised an eyebrow at that one. Maybe she didn't compare him, but he knew his Dad did. He just didn't measure up. Whenever he missed a few points on an exam, his Dad would say, "Where are the other two points? Why can't you focus more? Jesse never had any issues in English class." Or whatever class or sport. You take your pick. But no one cared that Jesse screwed up that night. They just ignored it and made him out to be some kind of hero.

"This discussion is over, Michael. You will call New York University and tell them no. And you WILL go to University of Maine this fall. End of story."

"I am going to NYU and forget about August. I am leaving tomorrow. And you are right about one thing, sir. This conversation is over." Michael's tone was self-satisfied and snide … and maybe just a little scared.

Marty looked at her husband and then at Michael.

"How do you plan on getting to New York? Where will you live? You're supposed to be working at the market the rest of the summer and you can't move into the dorms until the end of the summer anyway."

What Michael's mother was saying was all true. He knew she was trying to be reasonable but he just couldn't — not this time. He was always playing it safe. But he didn't want that anymore. He wanted a change.

"I'll figure it out," said Michael, trying to sound self-assured.

"Now listen, son," James said, trying to appear calm. He leaned both hands on the worn mahogany table and leaned forward. "You'll do what I say—"

"Or what, Dad?" Michael asked in an exasperated tone.

Whatever his father said wasn't going to change his mind. Nothing was going to change his mind. This was his chance. His chance to be his own man, to only have to measure up against his own self, not his brother, not his sister, not anyone but himself.

Michael leaned his own hands on the table and stared his father in the eyes, "What are you going to do?"

"That's enough! Michael, you apologize right now," exclaimed Marty.

"Marty, I'll take care of this," James said, as he nudged his wife back.

"So you really want to leave all of this that badly. Can't wait a few months; you can't wait to talk this through like a man. You're going to leave us and your responsibilities at the market with no notice. You just went ahead and did whatever you wanted without caring about the rest of us, huh?"

For a moment, Michael debated what to say next. Instead he just said, "Yes. I want to leave here that badly."

Before he could stop himself the words were out. They hung in midair and everything seemed to stand still for a moment. He debated whether to take the words back, or whether he even could. He couldn't though, because it wouldn't be true. But those thoughts quickly changed once his father spoke.

"You want to go off, son? Fine then, go right ahead. Be my guest. Just go. But I want you to remember this. If you walk out that door, you'll get nothing from us. No money, no tuition help, nothing … not even a goddamn Christmas card," said James, a self-satisfied and assured look on his face.

"Now just wait you two — let's take a little time to discuss this rationally. Calmly. This is all just getting a little out of ha—"

"No, Marty. No," James said with force.

"It's time Michael learned just how easy he has had it here. Boy, you go off, take off tomorrow for all I care. You've had a good thing here, but you aren't going to learn that till you are out of here. Hell, maybe you'll grow up a little. Maybe then you can call yourself a man."

Michael's palms were sweaty. It was really happening. He was really going to be leaving. He'd have to leave without his family's support, no coming home for holidays, no writing to ask for money if things got tough. It wouldn't be easy but he was going to do it. He'd be on his own. His own man.

"I don't need you, or your money. I can do this alone."

"Hah!" James cackled. "We'll see what you say in a few months, heck, maybe in a few days. You'll realize what you are throwing away, son. You might not see it now, but you will."

"No, I won't, Dad. I don't need you and I never will. I am never coming back here, not ever."

"Michael, don't say that this isn't your home, it always will be and I'll always be here for you," Marty pleaded, and shot her husband a look. A look that said 'not another word.'

His father said nothing more. He just wore a self-satisfied smile and was silent. He stood there in his "Malone's Market" shirt looking like he was above everything and everyone, especially his son. In that moment, Michael knew he was making the right decision. He couldn't stay in this house; he couldn't stay in Maine any longer. He was tired of being compared to his sister, his dead brother, the past and his father's dreams. He would never live up to them. But he would show them, he would succeed and he would never come back. His mother started to cry softly as Michael walked out. He couldn't look at her or he might change his mind.

As Michael walked away, Marty looked at James. He moved towards her and brought her into his arms and said, "He'll be back. This is where he belongs, he just doesn't know it yet."

CHAPTER ONE

The morning sky was glowing pink and the air smelled of salt. The low humming of Michael Malone's rental car seemed a little out of place as he pulled up the dirt road to a ramshackle house that looked like it was badly in need of repair. The Penobscot area was now known as one of Maine's most picturesque escapes. He stepped out of the shiny black Mustang coupe in a two-piece suit and necktie. They weren't Armani, but you could tell they were expensive despite the understated look. He halted in front of the faded red door of the sea-worn Cape Cod home.

"What happened to this place?" he mumbled as he stared at the worn shingles that were left clinging to the home. Definitely not picturesque, that's for sure, he thought. The cedar shingles were either missing or faded and worn beyond the usual salt grey that New England homes had become known for. It had been thirteen years since he'd been back home. It felt like forever and just yesterday all at once.

He was home. His skin prickled with goose

bumps and a sense of uneasiness spread through him. Instinct screamed at him to head back to the car and get as far away from Gray Harbor as soon as possible. But he had to be there for her, for all of them.

He had seen his mother and siblings periodically since his impassioned vow almost thirteen years ago never to return, but he had kept true to his words until now. He had not once come back since that fateful day. He had wanted to many times but felt like he would never be welcomed by his father after the blowout they had about Michael going to college in New York.

Since then his family, all but his father, had come to New York once a year after Christmas. He'd take them to Radio City, to the Russian Tea Room for High Tea, and, of course, to a New York City institution: Midtown Comics — a favorite of his little brother Jonah. During all that time, he had not once truly spoken to his father. And his father never once made an effort to reach out to Michael either, not on his graduation from undergrad, the completion of his MBA, or landing the job he had worked so hard to land. When Michael called home, his father would barely grunt and then just passed the phone off, completely ignoring anything Michael said to try to make things right. Now Michael took a deep breath, shut his eyes, and raised his hand to knock. Before he had a chance, the door flew open.

"I can't believe it you actually showed up," said Jonah, barely looking at him.

"Whoa, check out the car. What is that? It's wicked!" His brother, who was not so little anymore, was clearly more excited about the car than he was about Michael. Michael told Jonah it was just a rental and then put him in a headlock, for old times' sake.

"Jeez dude, no need to mess up my hair," Jonah exclaimed, and then he screamed "Mom, Annie, Judy … Mikey is here and he's trying to kill me!"

Mikey — It had been a long time since anyone had called Michael by his old nickname. Everyone in town had called him that, well, almost everyone. He stopped going by it once he went to New York. Michael had felt more mature than "Mikey." He felt almost silly thinking that now, though. He really didn't care either way now that he was an adult. Thinking about it, he could hardly believe he had left home when he was around Jonah's age. Jonah reminded Michael a little of himself. Jonah's six-foot frame and blue eyes mirrored Michael's. His dark hair was longish and swept to the side. He was tan and vibrant, in the way only twenty-year-olds can be. Jonah's "Malone's Market" t-shirt, worn jeans, and Converse sneakers were a contrast to Michael's clothing — and Jonah smelled faintly like fish. It served as a reminder of why Michael had not been back all these years.

Sometimes he felt like he had changed too much to come back. The calm of Maine inside Michael had been replaced. He was now an on-edge New Yorker. Michael mussed up his brother's hair one more time while Jonah struggled to get out of his reach. Michael remembered the day he left — Jonah was just seven years old. Michael had snuck into Jonah's room and promised that no matter what, he would always be his big brother and help him in any way he could. Michael tried his best to keep that promise. Although he couldn't be there in person, he called Jonah all the time on the cell phone he purchased for him and he was always available to give his brother advice when he needed it. When it came time for college applications, Michael edited all of his essays. Jonah was a smart, good kid who everyone loved. And like Michael, Jonah also was focused on his passion and his dream: computers. The only difference was that Jonah didn't totally follow his dream, which was to study computer science at Stanford. He did exactly what was expected of him and stayed in Maine. So did his little sister Judy. Michael had tried to be a good brother to Judy, too, but for some reason they had not bonded as much. It was probably because she was just four years old when he left.

"Glad you came. Mom was worried you wouldn't 'cause of your 'stupid pride.' And do not touch my hair again, it takes a long time to get it to look like this." Jonah smoothed his hair back and was about to say something else when their mother came to the door.

Behind her was Michael's older sister Annie, with Judy, who was no longer so little, trailing behind. She had just turned seventeen and Michael couldn't believe how much had changed since he saw her just last year when his family visited him in New York. Judy had grown so tall since last Christmas! She was at least five foot ten and had long black hair and blue eyes. She was gorgeous. He was both proud and worried at that moment ... he might need to beat up some boyfriends during this visit. He smiled at the thought. He always wished he and Judy could be closer. Maybe he could make some inroads toward that goal on this visit. He and Annie had also drifted apart somewhat through the years. He wasn't as up-to-date as he should be on her children or her home.

The whole family was there, except for James Malone. That stubborn old goat, as Michael's mother frequently called him, still hadn't forgiven Michael. But that's not why he wasn't there. It wasn't a choice James had made. Although Michael wondered if his father would be here to greet him if the circumstances were different. Now, he would never know.

"Mom! Jonah, Annie, Judy, I'm glad to be here." Michael hugged his teary-eyed mother.

She was short, with graying hair, and the same pale blue eyes that Jonah, Michael, and Judy all had. She had a few more wrinkles than the last time Michael saw her, which was just last November, for his birthday. She seemed to have aged beyond her fifty-four years. It had been a tough year for her with all that had happened to Michael's father.

"Come on in, Mikey, glad you're here. I only wish you could have seen him before it happened." Marty let out a cry and held Michael tighter.

Judy Malone touched her brother's shoulder and said, "Good to see you, bro," Then she looked to her mother. "Mom, why don't we all go inside."

Judy had a quiet maturity about her that was simultaneously comforting and disturbing. Having someone so young seem so together could be disarming. She steered them into the kitchen. It looked the same. Linoleum floors with a strange black octagon and white square pattern, oak cabinets with cast-iron pulls and 1970's 'modern' olive green appliances. The best part of the room, the large country farm table with faded red legs, was still there, and the picnic bench seat—perfect for numerous children to hang out on—was there, too. Michael, Annie, and Jesse had sat there all the time while growing up. It was there that they did their homework together, played Monopoly, shared after-school snacks, and just talked. He also remembered Jonah and Judy coloring and doing their art projects there when they were small children.

Michael remembered the time Jesse and he had carved their initials into the table top with their Dad's Swiss Army knife. They'd gotten so many lashes that their bottoms matched the table legs. He smiled at the memory. James Malone wasn't a violent man, but when they were small, he hadn't shied away from disciplining his children. Michael had been just eight years old at the time and Jesse twelve.

"Jesse." Michael sighed. Michael hadn't thought about Jesse and the night he died in a long time. The football team had just won the state championship so Jesse got to go to all of the victory parties and took Michael along with him. There was a lot of beer at the parties, and drugs. Jesse wasn't a big drinker… but that night he was drinking… he was drinking a lot. Michael had never seen anything like it. For the first time in his life, Jesse had decided to cut loose. He took shots, drank from a funnel, danced, and sang at the top of his lungs. Then the cops came and Jesse had to get out of there, and he and his girlfriend Jen headed for the car. Jen's little sister Beth had tried to convince both Jesse and Jen not to drive. Jen told Beth to back off and she got in the car. Just a few miles from the party, they ran into a tree. The car flipped over and neither survived.

Michael shook his head and looked beyond the kitchen into the dining room. He struggled with the memories of Jesse and that day with his dad over and over again in his head. Sometimes he wished he'd done it differently. Other times he wished his Dad hadn't been such a stubborn jerk. He couldn't change the past, but he was hoping there would still be time to change the future.

Michael walked towards the dining room. It still looked like a mess, even in the distance. He guessed they were still using it as an office, even though Jesse's room had been empty for years.

His mother's voice interrupted his thoughts. "So honey, are you hungry? I made a carrot cake just the other day, your favorite. And we have chocolate milk. I even bought that sparkling water you like so much. Dang, what's it called... San Pelican? Oh, well, whatever it is, what would you like to have?"

She was speaking so quickly, Michael didn't even know what to say.

"Okay, mom, let the man breathe, he just got here," said Annie. Michael shot her a look of appreciation. He thought to himself had it not been for Annie, growing up would have been a lot harder than it had been, even if she was a rat sometimes. Even though Annie was five years older, she and Michael had always had a connection. She'd always come over and 'save' him when things got bad. He was a bookish teenager with only a few friends and was often the butt of people's jokes. Sometimes Michael had felt really alone, especially after Jesse died, but then Annie would be there with popcorn and videos.

"Oh, I'm fine, Mom. A sparkling water would be great. No carrot cake for me right now, though. But I will try some later, if that's all right."

Marty got his water and then sat down at the table. They all sat there in silence for a few minutes but it didn't last long. Annie never could stand the quiet.

"Guess I'll just come right out and say it. We're really glad you came home, Mikey. Dad's in bad shape. We know things haven't been the greatest between you two..."

"Oh, hell, Annie. Michael, your Dad hasn't been doing so hot for a while now and we think this has been a long time coming. I didn't want to burden you with it but we're in a bit of trouble now that he's gone and had a stroke." Marty let it all out in what seemed like one breath.

"I don't understand — did something else happen? Before the stroke? When? Where? Why didn't you tell me? I don't understand." Michael's words came out in a rush. Even though he hadn't been home in all this time, it wasn't like he hadn't spoken with his family. They spoke every week, sometimes more frequently, and no one had said a word about his father having any health issues. And now a stroke, he knew that part. But had Michael known about his father being sick he might have come back sooner, he might have been able to help. Maybe he could have stopped this from happening. Who knows what could be different now, had he known.

He had to stop himself, his thoughts were racing.

Marty paused and took another deep breath. "Well, remember when you were graduating from your MBA? You were furious we couldn't come down to see you for graduation because we had to 'take care of inventory'? You had that crazy internship at that Goldfarb place they always talk about on the TV and you were so concerned about getting a good job that I couldn't do that to you. You were just twenty-five, and your father had his first scare... a heart attack... and I just didn't want to burden you, and neither did your father. It happened the day before you asked to speak to him..."

Burden him? What did they think of him? That he was some kind of unfeeling monster? Sure, he had been mad at his father all that time, but he didn't want anything bad to happen to him. Although he sometimes hated to admit it, he still loved his father.

Annie interrupted. "I told you he didn't want to speak to you 'cause I didn't know what else to say...he didn't want us to tell you..."

"He didn't want you to miss your graduation... I guess he was also afraid you wouldn't choose him... that you wouldn't come see him," said Marty with tears in her eyes. "He never said that, but it's the sense I got."

Michael was taken aback — he didn't know what to say. He remembered that day. He was so upset they wouldn't come see him and because of *inventory* of all things, he had thought. He thought to himself that the market was all anyone cared about and he promised himself that that would never happen to him — that he would never become so consumed by something. It all made sense now: the house's complete disrepair, Jonah's decision to go to a University of Maine instead of Stanford. Michael felt ashamed that they didn't think they could ask him for help before... but he also felt angry that they had hid this from him. Despite all their issues, he was still family. And despite his Dad's pushy nature, there had been good times too.

Michael remembered that when he and Jesse were children, their dad would take them fishing. Michael was a little scared at first, especially of the bait — of all the things to be scared of! Jesse made fun of him terribly, but his dad didn't. He just explained gently that there was nothing to be afraid of — the bait wasn't going to bite and hooking them was simple. Despite his temper, his dad could be oddly gentle sometimes, which was strange for such a big, burly kind of a guy. His dad was right about fishing. Since that first trip, fishing had become one of Michael's favorite pastimes.

It's funny, for a guy who didn't want to spend his life filleting fish, he sure spent a lot of his free time fishing. Even in New York. His only vacations were to go out to the Hudson Valley and fish. It was always a trek but afterwards, Michael always felt relaxed and somehow more balanced, something he seemed to be lacking in the other parts of his life. Maybe life wasn't all bad in Gray Harbor. Michael had some good times in the past, but maybe the sadness of Jesse's death clouded things a bit — that and Michael's blow-out with his father over moving to New York.

New York. New York was great... or it would be if Michael ever got to enjoy it. Michael had been burning the candle at both ends ever since he finished his MBA. Life wasn't the same anymore. And taking a "vacation" or a leave had been something he never did before. Sure he went away, but always just for a weekend, and often he was fielding calls, even when he was out fishing on a boat. But he knew his time at his company was coming to an end soon, so he figured why not take a break. He decided to help the family on the Goldfarb Funds' dime, while he was still employed by the company. He had so much vacation time built up that if they did let him go, they'd not only have to pay him a severance but they'd have to pay him for seven years of missed vacations, he thought.

With the economic downturn, things had taken a turn for the worse... and Michael was on the high end of the pay scale as a Managing Director and on the low-end of bringing in the money lately. Although he was in charge of his group, he didn't always have the final say on the decisions these days, which is why he was concerned. It may seem ridiculous to get rid of one of your most senior people... but he seemed to have lost his touch, his pulse on the market, at least according to them. Or maybe the money just didn't matter anymore.

He had a nice nest egg saved now... but he didn't want to permanently leave until he figured things out. He also didn't want to make it easy on them. He had to remind himself how he came to be the director when he was only twenty-six years old. He replaced the last director and turned things around at the hedge fund. Within two years, they had become one of the most well-known hedge funds in the country. Michael had appeared on the cover of Trader Magazine annually for being so successful.

But enough of that for now — he had to focus. The next three weeks he hoped to help his family, reconnect with his father, figure out his next steps, and then go back to New York, hopefully with a plan of action. When he listed it all like that it seemed unrealistic... but he needed to make it happen. Maybe he'd take a completely different direction with his life, while he was at it. Maybe he'd do something that mattered, something that would do good for a change. He chuckled to himself. Of course he knew things might not happen quite that neatly. That was always hard for him, since he was an organizer and a planner. He loved making to-do lists and checking things off. Perhaps not the personality one would expect for a top trader. He wasn't a risk taker, but a calculated decision maker.

"Hey buddy, you still there?!" Jonah was waving a hand in front of Michael's face. "Mom just asked you something."

"Huh, oh yeah, I'm sorry. I was thinking that things have changed so much since I've been here last," said Michael.

"What, like all your gray hairs and Jonah's voice," Judy said, as she let out a laugh.

Michael reached over and gave her one of his signature noogies. "Hey stop it, you're going to mess it all up."

What was it with his siblings and their hair? Geez.

"Okay, kids, settle down," said Marty. "What I was saying, Mikey, is I am so glad they let you get away at work. Will you have to take a lot of calls while you are here?"

"A few," he lied. "But hopefully not too many. It's been a long time since I've had a break—" Michael was cut off by Annie's snide tone.

"So, how long do we have the pleasure of your presence… one day, two days?"

Michael made a face at his older sister. "Three weeks."

When did she get so resentful? All through high school, Annie was off being irresponsible with Tom while Michael was stuck at home helping. He understood he had been gone for a long time, but he just didn't get it.

His mother perked up a little, "Three weeks! Well, that's great. I mean, of course we wish you could be here even longer, but three weeks will be a great help. As you can see, we've let a few things slide around the house, since your father got sick." She made a gesture with her hands and looked around the room before saying, "And the bills have been stacking up. With me running the market and the household, it's been a lot to take on. And Annie helps as much as she can but with the kids and her husband, it's a lot."

Michael hadn't seen the kids in a long while, or Tom, for that matter. Come to think of it, he hadn't received one of their traditional Christmas cards with the awful matching sweaters in a few years. Michael looked around then and saw that his mother's statement was … well, it was an understatement. He looked up at the ceilings and saw some water damage. The place needed a fresh coat of paint, and frankly… well, a good dusting. His mother had never let the house get this out of hand when they were growing up, and they were a rowdy crew. He'd never been terribly handy like his brother Jesse, but he was sure he could help somehow. He started to feel a little guilty all of the sudden. How could he have let this happen? He was making millions and he let his parents' home get to this point. He felt awful. He would help: he'd do whatever it took to make things right.

At that moment, Annie said, "You know, Michael, we could most use your help at the market. You know math was never my strong point and Mom and I haven't been able to keep up with everything there. I just feel like we're so behind on things there. Maybe you can help us get on track?"

His mother added, "Oh, and the bills for the house, too. You know where everything is—the dining room table, as usual. The checkbook, everything is there. We should have enough to cover things, but to be honest, since your father's stroke, I haven't really done much with it all."

Bills, organizing, now that sounded like something he could handle, and maybe he could pay someone to do the repairs or enlist his younger siblings. Not much of a vacation, but since when did he enjoy vacationing?

"That sounds great, I'd be happy to help take care of all that. And maybe Judy, Jonah, and I can make a plan for how we can maybe tackle some of the repairs around the house, too. How about it, Mom?"

At that moment, Marty got up from her seat and went around the table to give Michael a squeeze.

"I knew you'd come help us out if we really needed it, Mikey. We're so glad to have you here… and you know what? I think your Dad will be happy to see you came back to help us out."

Marty looked at Michael and seemed a bit choked up and had a faraway look in her eyes.

"Mom?" Michael said. He repeated himself. "Mom?"

"Oh, yes, I'm sorry dear, I was lost in thought. Why don't we get you settled? Judy, come now, chop chop! Why don't you walk Mikey up to his room and make sure you grab him some towels from the linen closet so he can wash up before dinner. It's going to be simple tonight, just some clam chowder."

That odd look on her face worried Michael. He got up and let Judy lead the way. They walked out into the main hall and walked up the long staircase. It still had the same faded green carpet that had been there when Michael was in high school. As they walked up the stairs to the room Michael would be sharing with Jonah for the next three weeks, it hit him. Michael could pay to get work done on the house, maybe a renovation was in order — it wouldn't make up for all the years he had lost with his family, but maybe it would make things just a little bit easier for them. Besides, what was a few thousand dollars anyway?

CHAPTER TWO

What was a few thousand dollars indeed. After a night of catching up with the family over his mother's New England Clam Chowder, a salad, and delicious carrot cake, Michael went to bed not really knowing what the next day would hold. His mother suggested he check out the 'home office' in the morning and maybe take care of some of the bills for her while she headed over to Malone's Market, and then later, they could both go to the hospital to see his father. He had no idea what he was getting himself into.

He had thought the house was in disrepair, but compared to his parents' finances, the house was looking like it was a pristine mansion all of a sudden. There were missed mortgage payments and utilities close to being shut off. Jonah's tuition bill was due in a few weeks, and despite his scholarship, it looked pricey. There was no way his parents' checking account could handle this. And it looked like James had taken a second mortgage out on the house. By noon, Michael had spent seventeen thousand dollars of his own money bailing them out. He could never tell his mother or his father, they had too much pride, but it had to be done. And frankly, he had been making over a million dollars a year for the past few years at the hedge fund, not including his bonuses, and he barely spent a penny because he was so busy and so focused on making more money.

He had this dream of making a lot of money before forty and retiring. He had made some great investments and accrued a lot of money the past few years since his MBA, but he lived pretty modestly. His colleagues always made fun of him because he was the only one who didn't have a car and who still bought his suits at Men's Wearhouse. The suits were actually still quite nice but couldn't be compared to custom suits or to what his friends were buying at the major design houses in New York. He dressed well; he just didn't think he needed to flaunt his money. He lived in a small alcove studio he had purchased years before in the West Village and frankly, he didn't accumulate much because there would be nowhere to put it!

His parents had always taught him to live within his means, but it seemed that he lived far below the means of someone who was a millionaire. But despite what he saw now in his parents' checkbook, what he had learned growing up stuck with him. Those lessons were a good thing. Now he could spend that money on something that mattered more than a sports car or fancy clothes — his parents. And in terms of his job… if he lost his job now he could probably retire if he lived modestly. He'd go crazy if he did, but he knew he could do it if he wanted to, or if he or had to.

He looked around. He had accomplished a lot

since he woke up at six that morning. By noon, the bills were paid, old mail and junk mail had been shredded and bagged, and the dining room looked at least a little more organized. No one would be dining in there anytime soon, but at the very least they'd be able to find what they needed. The rest of the house, on the other hand, could use some work. He looked out the window and saw that Judy was outside mowing the lawn. He waved and she waved back. Judy was hard at work, but where was Jonah? He walked outside and decided to chat with Judy before looking for Jonah.

"Hey, sis," he said, as he walked out of the screen door in the dining room.

She shut off the mower and came over to him, wiping some sweat from her brow.

"Hey, Mikey, what's up?"

"Do you always do the yard work?" he said, surprised that Jonah wasn't helping her out.

"Yeah, when Jonah went off to college I just kind of picked up a lot of the chores, and since he's been back for break I think he's still in college-land." She rolled her eyes.

Michael was thoughtful for a moment. "Have you started thinking about school yet?"

Judy looked at him and said, "Yeah, I have, but the schools I want to go to are so expensive and I just don't think I could even broach the topic yet, you know? Plus, I'd like to go away, but it just doesn't seem right... at least not now."

Michael understood. "Well, you have a few months before you start applying, anyway. If you want any help with your essays or anything let me know, okay?"

She smiled a little at that. "Sure, I'll keep that in mind for when I am ready."

Michael nodded. "Okay, well, I'm going to go look for Jonah... I'm guessing he's probably still asleep."

With that, Judy huffed a bit and said, "Of course he is," and went back to her chores.

Michael headed back into the house through the screen door and past the dining room and the kitchen. He walked back up the stairs toward his childhood bedroom, but first stopped outside Jesse's old room. He had wanted to go in last night, but couldn't bring himself to do it. He decided to go in and see what remained. The room was—clean. He couldn't understand it. The rest of the house was a complete and utter disaster, but not Jesse's room. It's like time stood still. Michael felt like Jesse could return at any moment and say, "Get out of here, pepperoni face, I have things to do."

Ahh, pepperoni face, just one of the lovely names Jesse had called him. Michael had almost forgotten it. Jesse lovingly gave him that nickname once Michael had hit puberty and pimples had taken over his face. Although everyone loved Jesse, he wasn't always the nicest — sometimes being so cool went to his head. Michael hated to think that, especially since Jesse was gone — but it was true. He shook himself back to reality and walked in. The carpet was a dark blue and the twin bed had a mission-style bed frame with a matching nightstand, dresser, and desk set. The same old blue and green plaid flannel sheet set that had been there when Jesse was in high school was still on the bed now. Jesse's trophies littered the dresser and his desk still had his books on it. This was surreal. What was going on in this house? And where the hell was Jonah?

Jonah was still sleeping, of course. What the hell, Michael thought. His mother and his sisters were busting their asses and this loser was sleeping the day away. Michael crept into the room quietly. It struck him that it looked exactly the same, well, save for the mess. This whole house was like a time capsule. He looked over at his side, where he had neatly made his bed. His old Wayne Gretzky posters were on the wall and even his science fair trophies were on the dresser. This room had been his alone until Jonah was born. Jesse had his own room and as the older of the two boys, sharing wasn't going to happen. Michael remembered begging Jesse to share with him so he wouldn't have to share with a toddler. No dice. So Michael got stuck sharing his room with Jonah. So instead of listening to the Dave Matthews band or other popular 90's music when Michael was a teen, he was listening to Barney and Friends on Jonah's pale blue boom box. As much as he hated it at the time, that experience had allowed them to stay close even though Michael had been gone all these years.

The room wasn't large but it was big enough for two twin beds, two dressers, and two desks that were situated in the middle of the room and acted as a divider. He was surprised Jonah never rearranged the room after Michael had left, and that Jonah had managed to contain his mess mostly to one side of the room. On Jonah's side there were computer parts everywhere. They even had begun to creep over onto Michael's old desk.

Jonah was always a tinkerer and loved computers.

In fact, Michael had bought Jonah his first one for his fifteenth birthday and ever since, Jonah had become obsessed with computers, programming, and games. Sure he was an athletic kid, he even played basketball in high school, but he truly loved computers. He probably spent a little too much time playing video games but he was mostly a good kid. A lazy one yes, but he was a 'good egg,' as his mother often put it.

Michael crossed the floor of the blue carpet to where Jonah was soundly sleeping. He leaned over and removed the top sheet. Jonah didn't stir. Michael then rolled up the fitted sheets quietly on each side. Jonah still didn't stir. Michael yanked the sheets up and dragged Jonah onto the floor with one swift movement.

"Hey, what's the big idea?" yelled a groggy Jonah. "Ouch … what the hell do you think you're doing? I was sleeping, for crying out loud!" Jonah's eyes were still shut during their exchange and he looked like he could fall right back asleep.

"Jonah, seriously. It's noon. I have been up for six hours working. What is your lazy ass doing with the summer?! Get up — we have work to do." Michael looked down at Jonah and suddenly noticed he was fully clothed. He even still had on his sneakers from the night before.

"What did you do? Stay up all night and play video games?" Michael was a little exasperated, especially since Judy had been up almost as long as Michael and she was hard at work.

"Oh, come on, I always do stuff, let me just sleep," Jonah said, as he fluffed his pillow and made himself comfortable on the floor. Michael leaned forward and grabbed Jonah's feet and dragged him into the hallway with his sheets and all, laughing the entire time.

"ALL RIGHT, ALL RIGHT! FINE, I'M UP," Jonah shouted. He didn't look happy. But this wasn't a happy time and he had to get to work; they all did.

"Good, we have work to do. Get dressed. We're going to the hardware store in town," said Michael, with determination in his voice.

Jonah grumbled but began to look for a clean shirt among the computer mess on the floor. Michael shook his head and walked out and began to survey the damage in the house. He wasn't going to remodel or anything crazy, he decided, but a fresh coat of paint on the walls and some cleaning would be good. He'd hire a maid service except his mother would kill him. In a small town like Gray Harbor, everyone would know that Marty had a cleaning lady come over 'cause she couldn't handle it. Michael had a feeling she wouldn't like that. Marty wasn't the type to admit she couldn't handle something. Neither was Michael. It seemed to be genetic.

Michael made note of how much paint he'd probably need and jotted down the colors he saw around the different rooms in the house. He also made note that maybe they should rent a carpet steamer and other cleaning supplies. He didn't have much time but he was going to get this project going.

"All right, I'm ready, but can we eat first? I'm starved," Jonah said, as he walked down the stairs.

"Why don't we go to the diner after we run some errands? My treat," said Michael.

"All right, sounds good," Jonah said, as he

yawned. "Want me to drive?" Jonah looked at Michael hopefully. He had been eyeing Michael's rental car, which was a black Mustang convertible.

Michael agreed and handed Jonah the keys. Jonah instantly perked up and bounded out the door. He was clearly excited to drive something other than his parents' old station wagon.

Jonah hopped in and put the keys in the ignition of the sleek car. "Man, this is sweet. Is this really a rental?" Michael nodded in reply.

"Too bad. Why don't you just buy one of these yourself? Don't you make like a bazillion dollars a year or something?" asked Jonah, as he pawed the vehicle.

"I don't really need a car in the city. I take the subway everywhere or take cabs, so having a car would just be an unneeded expense," explained Michael. "And I don't make a bazillion dollars, okay?" Michael looked at him pointedly.

"Man, you sure are boring for a rich dude. So are we are heading to McAllister's Hardware? They have changed a lot in the past few years. That store is really nice now. They have all this high-end stuff and even an interior decorator. I forget his name but Mom says some dude who works there knew you and Jesse when you guys were growing up…" Jonah continued you to chat about some more of the changes that had been made since Michael had last been home.

Michael got lost looking out the window. So much had changed. It's amazing what thirteen years and a surge of tourism could do to a place. Gray Harbor was no New York, but man, it sure had been cleaned up in the past couple of years. They drove by the many well-manicured Cape Cod and Victorian homes that lined the streets. They didn't look like tourist homes, either; they looked like year-rounders' homes. Some children's toys were scattered on a lawn. Families were playing outside together. A family. That's something that didn't seem possible for Michael in New York.

God, it had been months since his last date. Michael had had plenty of dates in the past. He was good looking and rich now, but at a certain point, going home with random women who didn't care about you, who only cared about your money, status and looks, no longer did it for Michael. He wanted something more out of his life. It was all beginning to feel really meaningless and contrived.

At first all of that had been fun, all the meaningless sex and the power. He hadn't had much luck with girls in high school. He had never even slept with a girl until college. He came close once in high school with his lab partner, Beth. She was a real brain and probably the only person he had liked from the popular group. Even after what had happened with Jesse and Beth's sister... well, knowing her, she had probably gotten out of this town, away from the memories. He imagined by now she was probably a doctor or a lawyer. As he returned to his thoughts of New York, he tried to think of one good friend he had. While he was struggling to think of a real friend he had made over the years, Jonah continued to rattle on and update him on all the things going on with his friends from home in Gray Harbor, his frat brothers at the University, and all the girls. He even mentioned there was one girl of interest from town, but it "wasn't serious or anything."

Michael tried to think of a story about him and

friends he had to tell his brother, but he drew a blank. Who did he have in New York? His colleagues, his secretary... his cleaning lady Marisol. That was it. What was he doing with his life? He had been blind with ambition all these years, but being at the top felt lonely now. He was just working, and working for people who didn't value him. After all, he was about to be replaced by a twenty-five-year-old Harvard grad. No one had said it yet but Michael just felt it. He had a sense for these things and for someone who made his living off of gut feelings about the market, that meant something. They passed the old Gray Harbor Lighthouse, and what looked like a fancy inn.

"Hey, Jonah, what is that place? Did someone buy the old Jameson house?" Michael asked, as he looked at the pristine old home. It had gray shingles and Adirondack chairs carefully placed on the well-manicured lawn. As Michael looked more closely, he saw a parking lot — how strange, he thought.

"Oh, yeah, that's the fancy place, the Warren Inn. It's a really popular bed and breakfast and a bar-restaurant. Or a tavern or whatever. Hey, maybe we can get in some night and watch the game and have a couple of beers?" said Jonah with a hopeful look.

"Maybe we can get some dinner there one night, but no beer for you till you are twenty-one, my friend, at least not on my watch." Michael had been careful about drinking ever since Jesse's death, and he was especially against underage drinking.

"All right, all right. You can't blame a guy for trying. Anyway, I heard it's really nice and they buy a bunch of stuff from the market all the time. I've done deliveries there before. Never eaten there, though, so that could be cool."

"Great, we will go. Maybe this weekend," said Michael. He looked at the Inn curiously. Maybe it could be a good place to spend some evenings the next couple of weeks to get out of the house. Living in New York, he was used to bars and restaurants for most of his meals. Like most New Yorkers, living in such a small apartment always made Michael crave space.

They drove a few more miles up some winding hills and past some more homes that looked more modern and empty — definitely vacation homes. It had been a long time since Michael had seen so many trees, he thought. He rolled down the windows and let himself breathe in the air, which was thick with the smell of pine. He let out a sigh. It was so different here. So much had changed. Growing up it had felt so small. It still was, compared to New York, but there was more around now, which was nice, Michael thought.

During the drive they passed two art galleries, an ice cream place, a small coffee shop, a diner, and a cute little bookshop. A bookshop, now that sounded like a fun business to run. Surrounded by books all day, talking about books — the nerd in him stirred. It sounded so much less stressful. Maybe that's what Michael would do in a few years when he retired, maybe even sooner. He could picture it now — a quaint little bookstore-coffee shop in the West Village.

"Here we are, McAllister's," said Jonah, interrupting Michael's thoughts.

Michael looked around and tried to take it all in. The place had changed a lot since he was a kid. It used to be a little rundown shack on its own private lot with a bait shop on the side. Now, it was a large whitewashed wood structure that had large planters in the parking lot showcasing plants you could buy out back in the greenhouse. Walking in the store, it felt extremely organized and even airy, like a small-scale Home Depot but with little hometown touches from Maine. Wood painted signs detailed what was contained in each aisle. In the front of the store, they even sold some trinkets for tourists, including Maine tartans, blueberries, maple syrup, and little moose decals for cars. The brothers made their way through the aisles, filling up the shopping cart with paint cans, brushes, and rollers.

"What happened to this place, Jonah? It's great," Michael said with an enthusiasm he thought he'd never express for a hardware store.

"Oh, some rich dude one of the McAllister ladies married, you know, whatever."

"Can I help you, sir?" said a tall, lean, well-dressed guy with red hair. He was definitely a few years younger than Michael, but he looked familiar. Michael just couldn't place him, but figured in such a small town, he had probably run into this guy at some point in his life.

"Um, yes." Michael looked at his nametag. "Yes, Robert, we'd love some help. I'm working on a home improvement project and was wondering if you had shingles here?"

"Hey, Mikey, I'm going to head off and talk to Billy. I'll come find you, okay?" Jonah said and walked off, not waiting for Michael's answer.

"All right, see you in a little bit, Jonah," said Michael, as he returned his attention to the store clerk.

"Ah, where were we? Shingles, I was asking if you had any?"

"Yes, we do have shingles. Can you describe what you're looking for exactly?" the man said.

Michael explained that he was looking for gray shingles for a small cape cod home by the sea. He detailed the location and even described the trim on the house. Robert seemed to be taking it all in.

"Oh, the old Malone place, yeah, I had been trying to convince the owner to repair it a while back, did you just buy it? That house has great bones. It could really be something with a little dusting off," he said excitedly.

"Oh, um, thanks and no, I didn't buy it. My parents still live there," said Michael.

"Wait. You're not Michael Malone, are you?" asked Robert.

Michael was taken aback — should he know this guy?

"Um, yes, yes I am. Have we met before?"

"Well, you probably don't recognize me. I'm Bob Adams. My eldest sister dated your brother," Bob looked serious for a moment, "He was a good guy. I know it's been a lot of years but I'm sorry for your loss."

Bob Adams. Jenny's little brother ... and Beth's. He could see the similarity but Michael didn't think they'd ever really officially met. Seemed like a nice enough guy, though.

"Oh, yeah, that's right, nice to see you, Bob. Thanks again and I'm sorry for your loss as well." There was an awkward pause, as Michael struggled for something to say. "What have you been up to?"

Bob had always been a nice kid. He was a few years younger than Michael, and Michael remembered some of Jesse's friends giving Bob a hard time when he was young. That changed once Jesse started dating Jenny.

"Well, I'm doing a little interior design, contracting here and there, and working here at the hardware store. It's been fun. Every day is different, you know?"

Michael nodded. Ahh, this must be who Jonah had mentioned.

"All right, let's talk shingles. So gray, you said?"

Michael nodded, "Actually, I have something specific in mind. Do you know the Warren Inn? I'm looking for something like that."

"Of course, sure, I know it well! I picked out all their furnishing myself actually, and they happened to purchase those shingles right here at McAllister's," he said with enthusiasm as he smiled proudly. They walked towards the back of the store and Bob pointed to exactly what Michael was looking for.

"These are them right here. But just so you know, they don't start out gray, they're more of a natural color and then they weather over time. Have you ever installed them yourself?"

"I hate to say this, but I'm not particularly handy," Michael admitted. He never liked to admit a weakness to another guy, but he wasn't about to pretend with the hardware store guy that he knew the first thing about shingles, home repair, or for that matter, which screwdriver was called a Phillips head. He also felt that Bob wouldn't care very much either way. He seemed very much like his own person, and that was something Michael had a lot of respect for.

"I'm not sure if you're interested in this, but we

do have an installation service here."

"That actually sounds perfect. Do you need to come out and do an estimate?

Bob smiled. "Yeah, I'll send someone over tomorrow morning. Let me just take down all your information and make note that these are what you want," Bob said, as he made notes on his clipboard. They made some small talk about sports, restaurants, and New York, while Bob was setting everything up. Bob was a big fan of New York but hated the Yankees and New York City cabs. The conversation was pleasant and he mentioned that Tuesday was a big night at the Warren Inn. Apparently they got a pretty big crowd when the Red Sox played. Bob said it was more of a wine crowd to watch the game rather than a regular pub vibe. He wasn't much into it, but he said the wine selection was great. That sounded exactly like what Michael needed. He wasn't a big drinker but he liked a nice glass of wine or even a beer every now and then.

Bob helped him with a few more purchases, including a doorknocker, a screen-repair kit, and the steam cleaner for the carpets. After thanking Bob for all his help, Michael went off in search of Jonah. This was perfect. He'd have things in order at his parents' in no time.

***

"So guess who I saw today," Bob said, as he pushed his way through the kitchen at the Warren Inn.

His sister Beth Adams looked up from her pastry dough and pushed a strand of hair out of her face before saying, "Who this time, Bob? Did the Ben

Affleck look-alike come to the store today?" She couldn't help but smile. Bob was always checking people out and telling Beth all about it.

"Oh, no, way better than him!" He paused for effect. "I saw Michael Malone at the hardware store!"

Oh, God, thought Beth. Michael Malone … Mikey ... she hadn't thought about him in years. She was still trying to forget him.

"Anyway, he's back in town and I helped him pick out shingles for his parents' house. He's doing some renovations there."

Beth couldn't believe it. He had left for college and never looked back. After Jesse's death, Michael had changed. She couldn't imagine what he was like now.

"Speechless much!"

Beth quickly snapped out of it. "Oh, shut up, Bob! I am not speechless. I was trying to remember the last time I saw him. And besides, I don't have the most positive memories when it comes to the Malones."

"Oh, please, you and Annie hang out all the time!"

"Bob, that's different. Besides, after what happened to Jen and Jesse ..." Her voice trailed off.

"Yeah, I guess I can see that ... too bad, things could have gotten a little more interesting around here, that's all," Bob said, as he left the kitchen.

But that wasn't all. Her sister's death was only part of it. The worst part of it. But her feelings for Michael were ... complicated.

CHAPTER THREE

Michael couldn't believe it was only Sunday night. He had only been home since Friday, but it already felt like he'd been there an eternity. After leaving the hardware store, he and Jonah went to the diner and got a bite to eat and then headed home. They set down drop cloths and prepared to paint the next day. Michael and Jonah steam-cleaned the rooms in the house that weren't being painted. It was starting to look good. While they were doing that, Judy dusted, took out the growing recycling pile, and even cleaned the draperies. By the end of it all, the three of them were exhausted and were cleaning out the contents of the refrigerator by eating anything and everything in sight.

At that moment, Michael's mother walked in with bags of food. "Hey, kids, help me with these bags. I brought home a few things for dinner. We're going to keep it simple tonight — just some rotisserie chicken and some salad fixings."

"Aww, come on mom, I'm a growing boy. If I keep eating this chick food I'm going to start to grow boo—" at that moment, Michael kicked Jonah hard under the table. Jonah bit his lip and glared at Michael.

"Sounds great, Mom, we're famished."

"Famished, eh? Well I can tell … what happened to this place?" Marty finally noticed the paint cans lined up on the wall and walked into the hall and saw the freshly cleaned green carpets. "Oh, wow, I forgot these carpets were even green, it's been so long since I could tell." She looked around at her kids, and she was glad they were all here together. And she was glad Michael was helping keep things in order.

She was tired, too, so this was a nice surprise. It had been a long day. She had run quickly to the hospital to see James on her way home from the market. He wasn't himself, he was struggling. The nurses said he was improving but that he had such a temper! Ahh, her James had always had a temper. But he also had a gentle way about him, and it pained her to see him hurting. James always had the last word. Hell, he always had the first. That was part of the reason she loved him so much. There was never a dull moment with James, that was for sure. Sure, sometimes his pig-headedness was tough, but there wasn't another man out there who cared more for his family than James. But for a man of so many words, there were two that didn't seem to be in his vocabulary.

She knew James was sorry about the things that had happened between Michael and himself, but he just never had the words to tell his son. He was just so Goddamn stubborn. She also knew he was proud of his son. He was proud of what Michael had accomplished. He had never told Michael that he was proud of him, but she knew he was. Whenever they were out and would bump into friends, they would ask about Michael. James would interrupt Marty before she could even speak and tell everyone his son was trader of the year, a big hedge fund manager in New York and an MBA, who would have thought a Malone with an MBA. Michael was the first member in the family to go to graduate school, that was a point of pride for James.

James hadn't spoken a word tonight, just grunted hello. And now she feared he never would. He looked miserable. The nurses said he would recover, but he would never be 100 percent. He really needed to put in the work to get better, but something was holding him back. Perhaps tomorrow she would get all the kids to go, maybe that would perk him up. And besides, it was about time that he and Michael confronted their issues. Although it scared her to think of it, she was worried they might not have much longer to patch it up. She was worried that if he and Michael didn't patch things up now, when something so big and life changing had happened, that they might not ever.

She made small talk with the kids while she put together dinner. Judy took down the plates and began to set the table. She was such a good kid, her Judy, but a little on the quiet side. She was a mix of Michael and Jesse, she thought. She had Jesse's startling good looks and Michael's quiet manner and smarts. That girl would go far if she let herself, but hopefully she wouldn't sacrifice as much of herself as Michael had. You could see it weighing on him whenever he walked into a room. Such a serious boy — such a serious man. God, the time flew. She really wanted to get Michael alone so she could speak to him about James and about their situation, but she couldn't seem to get him away from the others.

They all sat down and ate and exchanged pleasantries. Jonah relayed the story of how Michael got him out of bed that morning and they all had a good laugh. After dinner Michael, Jonah, and Judy did the dishes and Marty headed to the den. They soon followed in with popcorn and they all sprawled out on the couches and the floor to watch television. All the chairs were full except the lazy boy chair James always sat in. It had always been his chair and his alone.

"Kids, I saw your father today," Marty said. Everyone grew quiet.

"He's looking a little better. I could tell because he looked like he was going to kill his nurse half the time." She chuckled a little, remembering the looks he had given the nurse earlier that evening, "So I think he'll be back to his usual self in no time." She attempted a happy expression and hoped she both looked and sounded convincing.

"That's great, Mom," said Judy. "Can we maybe go see him tomorrow?"

"Yes, of course. Visiting hours end at eight o'clock, so why don't we head there after work? Maybe you can all pile into Michael's car and meet me there?" Marty looked around the room and her eyes rested on Michael. He looked uneasy, but she was waiting for his response. It was time he stopped being a coward and went to see his father. Enough was enough. She knew it hadn't been more than a day and a half, but she had hoped he would have taken the initiative and gone there today on his own.

Granted, she knew he had done a lot around the

house and had all sorts of plans for repairs to the place—which she appreciated, of course—but it was time. It was time for Michael to face his father, and maybe it was exactly the kind of boost James needed to get him motivated to work harder to get better. Marty was counting on it as she looked more intently at her son.

Michael felt like she was boring holes through him. No getting out of this one, he thought. "Sounds good, Mom, and maybe we can pick up some burgers or something from the Dairy Barn on our way home and maybe even a movie."

Michael took a pause and then said, "Not that I don't love broadcast television but I bet we can find something fun to watch while we're hanging out after we see Dad tomorrow? What do you guys think?"

Judy nodded, and Jonah said,

"Yeah, cool, and maybe we can rent the new Call of Duty video game? It's supposed to be awesome!"

"Sounds good," Michael said with forced enthusiasm.

Marty tried to relax, settling in on the couch next to Judy and staring blankly at the television. All of the stress was weighing on her. She had had a sense that James was hiding stressful news, but she couldn't be sure. Maybe with Michael here, she'd get down to the bottom of it and James could come home and not be so stressed anymore. She hoped. She let out a sigh and shut her eyes. She was trying to control her feelings of anger. Maybe this would all work out after all?

She was at least hopeful now and she had to admit the house did look a lot better today, and she was grateful that Michael had taken a look at all those bills.

James had always handled all of those things in the past and with him in the hospital these past few weeks, she had no idea how to make heads or tails out of their finances. And with James being in the hospital she was sure that the bills would just keep piling up. Same thing at the store.

Marty looked stressed. He didn't blame her, of course. This was a stressful time. But he felt like she was hiding something. And he was worried that he didn't know the extent of the problems going on here. Something was up and he wasn't even sure his mother knew the whole story. Now that he'd taken a look at the house books, he knew it was time to do what he promised Annie. He'd head over to Malone's Market tomorrow and see what he could do. With that second mortgage out on the home, he knew something was up, and he didn't like the feeling he had. He had avoided it today, but he just knew Malone's Market needed help. He just didn't know why it was in the position it was, or how exactly to fix it.

CHAPTER FOUR

Michael couldn't sleep all night. He kept thinking of his father and replaying their argument over and over again in his head. He tossed and turned. He kept thinking about his father's heart attack a few years before, and his stroke now. What if it was too late to patch things up? What if his father didn't want anything to do with him? His father was a stubborn man, but then again, so was Michael. He hadn't come back in all this time. With so many heavy thoughts weighing on his mind, Michael finally managed to fall asleep in the wee hours of the morning.

He woke up the next morning and struggled with what he would wear that day, and with facing the day in general. Michael didn't want to look uppity, but he also wanted to show his father he had changed. Then he stopped himself. His father just had a stroke. It was doubtful he would care about Michael's outfit. Michael finally threw on a Polo shirt, jeans, and brown Sperry Topsiders boat shoes. He combed his hair and looked in the mirror. His brown hair was perfectly in place, his blue shirt brought out the color of his eyes, and his muscular arms looked tan. He seemed strong and confident, but he was shaking on the inside. Not only was he going to see his father today, but he was also going to Malone's Market.

Michael looked over at the other bed, where Jonah was still asleep. He walked over but before he could say or do anything, Jonah said, "Don't even think about it, I'm getting up anyway. I have to go to the market today for work, and yes, I know those shingle guys are coming any minute."

With that, a sleepy Jonah got out of bed and made a beeline for the bathroom. He shouted over his shoulder, "Hey, I'll drive today if you want. I'll be down in five minutes."

Michael walked down the stairs and was glad in a way that with Jonah going in today, it would keep Michael from making a run for it, which is what he really wanted to do. As he walked down the stairs, the doorbell rang. It was a man from the hardware store. Michael let him in and they made small talk as Michael followed him outside to explain what he was looking for. The man took some measurements, scribbled down some calculations, and told Michael he'd have an estimate out to him no later than the next morning. If all was satisfactory, he could start the following Monday. They shook hands and he was on his way. After the man left, Michael stayed outside and walked around the yard.

Michael sat on a tree stump that was on the perimeter of the front yard and looked out at the street and back to the house again. This house held so many memories for him — both good and bad. But as he thought about it, the bad outweighed the good—his brother's death and his estrangement from his father. He sat there for a long while, lost in thought.

"Hey, Earth to Michael, are we going to go or what?" Jonah asked in an impatient tone.

"Oh, yeah, sorry. So what's the rush, little brother?"

"I don't like to be late, the guys at the counter will give me hell. That's all."

Michael looked at his brother with amusement. He suspected it was more likely that there was a woman of interest at the market, but he'd let it slide for now. "All right let's go. Here, you drive," he said as he tossed the keys up to Jonah. Jonah caught them, let out a whoop, and made a mad dash for the car. Michael trailed behind him.

Malone's Market wasn't far from his parents' house, just a fifteen-minute drive. It was also just a short distance from the Gray Harbor Lighthouse and the Warren Inn. When they pulled up to a house, Michael didn't recognize it at first.

Where were they, he wondered?

Then he realized in disbelief that this place was actually his family's market. It reminded him a lot of McAllister's, with the wood exterior, but instead of the whitewash, it was left natural with blue accents, reminiscent of the sea, no doubt. They still had the same old signage, which could use some updating, but overall the place looked great. They got out of the car and Jonah said he had to run and get started with work, but he pointed Michael towards Annie's direction.

Annie was the Assistant Manager at Malone's Market, and their Dad was the General Manager and Owner. Mom helped with operations in general but was sometimes out on the floor of the market as well. Michael saw Annie, who was wearing her blue Malone's Market t-shirt.

"Hey, Annie! Wow, this place looks so different," Michael exclaimed, trying to show enthusiasm.

"Yeah, before Dad's stroke he had started to implement all of these changes to the market. We're not done yet but it certainly is looking better. With all the tourists we're getting in Gray Harbor these days, we're trying to keep up. But frankly, with Dad out we put a halt on all updates till he's back ..." her voice faltered and then trailed off.

"Makes sense. Do you have time to give me a tour? Then you can tell me where you want me." He grinned at his sister. She was always good at telling people what to do, kind of like their father.

She walked him through what was now a small grocery area, which carried local produce, including blueberries — after all, it was Maine. There was another area with some basic staples like pasta sauces and canned goods, including canned anchovies, sardines, and salmon. They then walked through the fish market, which is where Jonah worked, and was once where both Jesse and Michael had worked as teenagers. The selection was huge, and a lot of it was local. Annie explained that they still bought from the local fisheries but now they did it in greater volume. The only problem was they couldn't always sell as much as they bought. They were still figuring out a system for that. They then walked through another new area of the store, which featured specialty cheeses and an olive bar. The place needed some more work but Michael was impressed; it almost felt like Dean &

Deluca in New York. But he did notice that many of the shelves had yet to be filled and that certain areas still looked like they needed organizing.

"All right, and just before the cashiers and that lovely empty space back there, are the stairs up towards office," said Annie, as she led him to the steps.

As they walked up, Michael observed that the stairwell itself also needed considerable work. In many places, there was just sheetrock up on the walls. They walked through a narrow corridor and up a wheelchair ramp. Wheelchair ramp? Then he noticed the elevator.

"We have an elevator, Annie?"

"Well, it's not done, but yeah, Dad was putting it in for when he and Mom are older, so they can get around a little more quickly."

Wow, Michael thought. Putting in and maintaining an elevator was going to be expensive. And heating and cooling the market probably wasn't cheap—It was three times the size it was when he was growing up. He was bracing himself for the inevitable — looking at the books.

"Why not put an office in that empty space downstairs instead?"

"I'm not sure what Dad had planned for that space, but that would make sense, wouldn't it? Okay, here we are, Dad's office," Annie said, as she led him into a room strewn with papers.

"Oh, my GOD, Annie what happened in here?"

She chuckled and gave him a lopsided grin before saying, "It's been a long time for you, huh? Dad is the most disorganized person under the sun. He's a great fishmonger, but a secretary, he is not. I could never make heads or tails of his filing. I don't know if less three weeks is going to be enough to fix this, but have at it!"

"Well, what do you want me to do?" Michael asked, slightly afraid.

"Well, you may have noticed outside of the fish we are a little low on inventory, which is affecting the number of customers coming in. What usually happens is I give Dad my order and he handles the rest. But we're behind on bills, so see if you can find our checkbook. The corkboard over there has a list of supplier information and our account information. That was my small attempt at getting things organized."

"All right, well, I guess I'll start sorting things out today and tomorrow I'll tackle orders and bills, how does that sound, captain?"

"Sounds good, skipper, now stop wasting time and get started." She winked at him and then left.

This was a bigger mess than he had imagined. Taking care of this office could take weeks alone. It looked like his father had just thrown the papers up in the air and said the hell with it all. Michael started by opening the file cabinets to check them out. They were either empty or stuffed with stacks of paper with no discernible order to them. Michael found a notebook and made a list of to do's in the office itself and then he came up with a potential filing system idea: Accounts Payable organized by Month, Suppliers, Purchase orders, Inventory Information, Human Resources Files, Payroll, and many more. He was starting to feel good. Now that he had a system, he knew he could start to get the place organized and frankly, it was nice to feel needed here at Malone's.

He knew he shouldn't be surprised but he hadn't

heard anything from his office in New York yet and it made him feel certain the end was near. He had left a message for Cindy, his assistant, but had received no response. Cindy usually called back minutes after he left a message. But he couldn't let himself think of that and what it all meant now.

Four hours had passed before he knew it, and he felt like he had began to make somewhat of a dent. Things were now organized in neat piles on the large table against the wall at the far end of the office. He had stacks of all of the employee and human resources information pretty much settled, as well as supplier information, and of course, a few other miscellaneous items. He was so focused on the task at hand that at first, he didn't even notice his mother come into the room.

"So, I see Annie has you knee deep in your father's files?" Marty's voice startled him and he looked up from the piles.

"Yeah, I don't really know what all of it means yet, just trying to get it organized today and probably tomorrow, and then I'll tackle it all — bills, and inventory, and whatever else you need." He looked at her and he felt good. He felt appreciated and like he was contributing. His mother's expression seemed to relax.

"Well, you must have worked up an appetite, why don't you follow me downstairs and I'll fix us up something to eat," she said and started heading for the door. Michael followed her through the long hall and down the stairs. She took him through the cheese market and waved to a beautiful young lady manning the counter.

"Margaret, good to see you, dear!"

She led Michael to the fish market and headed to the counter.

"Jonah, get the lobster I set aside out for me, ok?"

"Sure thing, Mom. Oh, and can you make me one too?" Jonah asked. "I break in thirty minutes."

Marty replied with only a nod and a smile, as her youngest son handed her the package.

"So, what do you say Michael? Follow me out to the back?"

"To the parking lot?" asked Michael, confused.

"Well, eventually yes, but I mean out back to the storeroom first, so I can make us some sandwiches," she said in an even tone.

Michael could tell something was weighing on her; she wore it on her face. They walked to the storage room, which had refrigerators and freezers, shelving, some counter space, and stairs that led to the basement, which Michael guessed housed more storage. It all looked really professional and high-end. His mother grabbed some rolls from one of the refrigerators and began prepping a simple lobster roll. She always had a way of making it with just a tiny bit of butter that was unlike any others he had ever had. Michael had been to tons of fancy places in New York and none of them compared, and, of course he couldn't think of a better one in Maine, either.

Everyone else in the area seemed to go a bit overboard with mayonnaise, well, except for Shaw's Lobster Shack, of course. Michael ventured that his mother's "Lobsta Rolls" rivaled even theirs ... they might even be better. She handed Michael a roll and then headed back to the fridge. She placed an extra roll in it for Jonah and grabbed two sodas.

"You still a fan of ginger ale?" she asked.

"Of course," Michael responded with a smile and graciously accepted the can.

"All right." She looked at him and sighed. "Let's head out."

They walked out of the storeroom and then took the back door, which deposited them on the side of building. There was small patch of grass there and a couple of large rocks overlooking the parking lot. They sat down silently and Marty began to dig in. They sat in silence for a while and enjoyed the rolls.

"So, have you figured it out yet?" Marty asked, her voice quivering a bit. When Michael looked at her face, it seemed that tears threatened her eyes.

"Figured out what, Mom?" Michael asked.

She looked at him a little surprised. "Michael, your father never told me, but I know we are in dire financial trouble. Look at the house, look at this store. I mean, it could be lovely, all of the improvements your father wanted to make ... but I think we're in over our head."

"Mom, I—"

"Michael, let me finish, okay?" she said with urgency.

"The night your dad had the stroke, he had been trying to make order of the office. He and I had a fight. I told him he was in over his head and that we needed help. I suggested we call you. You've always had a head for numbers and you work in finance, for God's sake. He started screaming and then throwing papers everywhere. I stormed out and when he didn't come home that night, I just thought he slept in his office.

Something he has been doing more frequently lately
…"

Michael couldn't believe what he was hearing. But it was all starting to make sense. The house was a wreck, Dad probably wasn't home much, leaving it all to Mom, while he tried to make his dreams come alive. But it almost cost his father his life and his family. Michael had to do something. He didn't know what yet, but something needed to be done.

His mother continued. "… I came back early the next morning to try to talk to your father. I wanted to talk it through with him and apologize for yelling. Ever since those McAllisters renovated their store, he's had this idea in his head that a little market like ours wasn't enough. But unlike us, the McAllisters have a lot of money behind them. Dana McAllister's husband is an attorney, so they had a lot of their own money to put into the business. Anyway, your father saw what they've done and wanted to make Malone's a destination, too. Problem is that now we have a second mortgage on the house, and fewer people shop here, well, because, well … you saw it in there … I just don't know what to do." She began to cry.

Michael hugged her and said, "Mom, I had no idea."

He didn't know what else to say. He knew Annie certainly couldn't help any more than she already was doing. Raising three kids and having a husband constantly being deployed overseas wasn't an easy life … and certainly not the most lucrative. Jonah was just a college student, and Judy was still just a high school student. Michael couldn't do this either … but he certainly could bail them out — if they would let him.

Paying the mortgage was one thing though, but Malone's market was another thing. Malone's Market was his Dad's pride and joy and something he had refused to be a part of up until now.

"I didn't want to bother you with it, Michael. I could sense something was going on with you, too. But this time I need you. I just can't do this alone anymore. Annie and the kids are great but I can't share this with them. But I also can't shoulder this guilt or this knowledge alone anymore."

She paused and looked straight into Michael's eyes. "Don't worry, I'm not asking you to move back here, Michael. I see the look of worry in your eyes. But I am asking you to forgive your father and understand him. He knew he couldn't do this alone forever and that's why he wanted you, Annie, and Jesse to be a part of Malone's Market."

Michael looked at her, unsure of what to say. Not this again. It wasn't his dream. Hell, he wasn't sure what his dream *was*, anymore.

"Your father has too much pride to ask you for help, Michael … and too much pride to ask for your forgiveness, so if you can't apologize for your part of it, just try not to upset him today when we go to the hospital. He's nervous about seeing you and he probably wants to pretend that nothing is wrong … just go along with that for now. It's all I ask."

She looked so sad and defeated. Michael was stewing inside a little about what his mother had said, but couldn't let it show. She clearly thought the way he handled things all these years had been wrong. Maybe she was right. But he still didn't like this. He had always hated confrontation. He couldn't do it when he was eighteen and preparing for college, and even now he hadn't been able to confront work with the fact that he knew they were going to get rid of him, and he'd been avoiding this visit for the past thirteen years. He had to stop running away. No matter how scared he was to face his father tonight, he would do it. And then he could stop being scared of what would happen if he saw him again, because he would have made the choice to go and speak with his father and be the bigger man and end this. Even though the past few days had been tough, they'd also been nice. He felt like he was getting to know both Judy and Jonah in a new light. And he also felt like his mother was finally treating him like an adult, by telling him how she really felt. He sighed.

"Mom, I'm sorry for everything that's happened. I know I didn't handle things very well when I left Maine for New York. There were so many times when I wanted to come back, but I wouldn't let myself. I couldn't let Dad be right. But I don't know what that's accomplishing anymore. I don't care about being right anymore, or who's right and who's wrong. It doesn't matter anymore. I want to help anyway I can. Any way you'll let me. And I will be on my best behavior tonight when we go see Dad."

She looked at him skeptically but smiled stiffly and said, "Okay, then. Well, let's get back to work, Mikey!" She rose and Michael followed.

Michael went back to the office and sat in his father's chair. It was the only imposing item in the office. It was a large, overstuffed leather chair on wheels, like ones you'd see in a law office. He sat in the chair and let the weight of his mother's words sit with him. He had to stop letting things just happen. It was like he was fourteen again. He had taken a firm stand only once in his life, and it didn't sit well with him. But now he was going to do the right thing. But first he had to see how bad things actually were at Malone's Market and he had to see if he could salvage his relationship with his family. For the first time his career was going to take a backseat to this rest of his life — and he liked the way that felt.

CHAPTER FIVE

Michael was infuriated. He had never encountered anyone more stubborn or ridiculous in his whole life. He had gone to the hospital earlier that evening with his Mother, his siblings, and even his nephews, to see his father. Needless to say, it didn't go well. His father was in bad shape but even with half his body being immobile, and even dressed in a skimpy hospital gown, he still looked imposing. Michael played the exchange over in his head as he drove around aimlessly in Gray Harbor.

His father had been sitting up in his bed, his left hand clutching his right in his lap, with a bored look on his big face. His skin looked gray, and although he looked weak, you could see he was a strong man. You could also see a little bit of Jesse in his eyes and that strong Malone chin and jawline. Marty said to James, "Look who's here, James. Mikey is in town to visit and he's been a big help at the market and around the house this week." Marty put on a smiling face as she addressed her husband.

"Hi, Dad," Michael said tentatively.

His Dad chose not to respond to him. Instead, he turned to Marty and struggled to get the words out, "I wanta you ta ta tell your son he's not welcome here. I'm tired."

Marty's face fell. "James ..." she said pleadingly.

"No, Mom, it's okay. I should have known better." Michael's anger was building and his face began to get red.

"Dad, I understand that I'm not your favorite person in the world, but I care about this family and about you, and I'm here to see you. And I'm here to help if I can. I'm sorry it took so long for me to come here." There. He had said it.

His father appeared to be listening. Michael could see it in his eyes. Or, at least he thought he saw something in his eyes. He thought James was going to address him, but instead, James stammered and said with some difficulty, "Marty, it's late. Why don't you all justa leave."

Michael shook his head and then stormed out of the room.

A few minutes later, Marty shepherded everyone else out of his room. Michael drove them all home in silence. They picked up some food from the Dairy Barn but Michael opted to spend the rest of the evening alone. He just didn't want to talk about it all. After he dropped everyone off, he just started driving.

***

He must have circled the block at least fifty times, and somehow he ended up at the Warren Inn. He had heard that they had a decent bar and decided that it might be just what he needed tonight. A drink and someplace where he could just forget everything that had just happened. He drove past the Inn's sign, and past its Adirondack chairs, and then parked in the lot. Looked like it was a slow night so far … probably typical for a Monday, he supposed. New Yorkers made every night a drinking night, but that was not the case in Maine.

He got out of the car and checked his reflection in the window of the driver's side. He looked presentable in his polo shirt from the morning and his jeans. He mussed with his hair a bit and decided to leave on his driving glasses. He usually wore contacts, or walked around a bit blurry, but he felt most comfortable in his designer tortoise shell glasses. When he was younger, he always felt like his glasses were really a mask behind which he could hide. Tonight, he felt like he wanted to hide away from the whole world. He breathed in and walked to the front of the Inn, looking for an entrance to the Tavern.

He walked to the reception area to ask about it. He looked around. The place looked great. It had a lovely fireplace and big comfortable blue upholstered French Country chairs with a worn mahogany wood. On his right was a small gift shop, which was really an alcove with Maine-centric trinkets. Just beyond the gift shop was the reception desk. Bob Adams from McAllister's really had done a great job with this place. Michael inquired about the bar and discovered there was an outdoor side entrance but that it was accessible from inside the Inn, as well. He walked down the corridor to the left as he was directed and came upon a quaint bar and restaurant area. It had chunky wood tables and chairs and a full bar with old fashioned 'milking style' wood bar stools and a large mirrored wall behind the bar. The rest of the walls were plank wood, giving it the feel of a ship. There were even little models of boats on the large stone hearth that was in the center of the room. There was one large flat screen television in the corner.

Michael made his way over to the bar. It was pretty quiet inside. There were a few people dining at the nearby tables and only one other gentleman sitting at the bar on the opposite end of where Michael decided to plant himself. He wasn't feeling in the mood for chatting it up with a stranger tonight. He just wanted a drink, a burger, and some television. As he settled into his stool, he leaned back to look at the specials on the board. He didn't even notice that a woman had walked over and was looking at him expectantly from behind the bar.

***

Beth felt like an idiot. She hated working behind the bar. People didn't treat her like she owned the Inn then. Not that everyone had to know it but she worked really hard to get here and had really pulled herself up. She always got annoyed when she had to cover shifts for her employees and people treated her like the hired hand. And what was worse, she had to serve this guy. She was hoping he'd order something simple. Although she was a gourmet chef, she couldn't mix a drink for her life. And oddly, something else made her a little uncomfortable around this man. He looked terribly familiar and he was good looking in that handsomely imperfect kind of way. His glasses also made him look bookish, not something that was common in Gray Harbor.

"What can I get for you, sir?"

Michael was startled by her presence and stumbled over his words. "Um yes, I'd just like a Sam Adams," he said, before he even registered to whom he was speaking. Then he really noticed her, all of a sudden. Wow, he thought. She was gorgeous. He had always had a thing for redheads ever since — no, it couldn't be ... could it?

She went to the fridge and breathed a sigh of relief. Thank God, a beer. That she could handle. She opened the beer with her back facing him and grabbed a menu as well.   "Here you go, sir, one Sam Adams. Can I interest you in something to eat?" She held out the menu.

As he accepted it, he thought to himself that she could interest him in a lot of things. Before he could let his mind wander or embarrass himself with a physical reaction to her, he said, "Sure, that would be great."

He quickly glanced at the menu and asked her, "What's good here? I came here thinking I wanted a burger but it looks like you have so much more to offer here."

Was he hitting on her? Seriously? Here we go. Why did men always hit on waitresses or bartenders? It's not like they actually want to chat with them. I mean, he was good looking, extremely good looking. She was taking way too long to respond to him and was just staring. She caught herself and was glad she had plenty of answers to his question. After all, the menu was her creation.

"Well, with that beer I'd recommend either our burgers or you could try the American Kobe flat iron steak with spring pea shoots, hickory smoked bacon, and roasted yukon gold potatoes with a tarragon whole grain mustard sauce."

She was sure he wouldn't get that, no one ever ordered something like that to just eat at a bar alone, but he did.

"Wow, that sounds perfect." He looked down at the menu again and added, " I'd also like to get the roasted Penobscot bay oysters … sounds great. I don't think I have ever had them served with a spinach shallot crème fraîche. But it sounds amazing," he said, as he pushed his glasses up his nose and beamed, handing her back the menu.

Beth noticed his movement and made the connection. She had seen him before. Her old lab partner always was doing that with his glasses whenever he smiled up at her. Well if it was him he had certainly changed for the better since high school. Back then he had been scrawny and quiet, with terrible acne and huge glasses. He was certainly looking better. She had never admitted it to her friends, but despite all that, she had had a little bit of a crush on him in high school, even though he was a bit of a nerd and short. He was always pleasant and had seen her at her worst and never mentioned it to anyone. When her parents had died, she broke down and Michael had comforted her and covered for her in school. And then not sixth months later, her sister, she — well, no point in thinking about that now.

"You're not Michael Malone, are you?" asked Beth.

Michael was taken aback; he was sure she wouldn't remember him. "Um, yes, yes I am. Have we met before?" He tried to play it cool. If this was Beth, she had changed quite a bit herself. She was stunning, even in her bartending getup. But it just couldn't be. Looking at her now ... could it be?

"It's me, Beth Adams. You know, from chemistry in high school."

Beth Adams. It was her. He couldn't hide his surprise, although he felt like an idiot because he knew this was a possibility. In high school Beth was still tall and thin ... in fact, she had towered over Michael, who didn't seem to hit his growth spurt until college. She had always been nice to him back then, although he always felt a little uncomfortable around her. And he was starting to feel little uncomfortable around her now. He had had a crush on her in high school, ever since they were lab partners freshman year. He always liked the look of her and he loved her hair ... and she wore thick glasses that let him forget that she was popular and that ... well, that he was so far from it. Nothing like Jesse.

Being in school as a freshman the same time Jesse was there had been hard for Michael. Jesse was probably the one who kept Michael from getting beat up, but when people found out he was Jesse's brother, they thought he was going to be athletic, or funny or cool ... yet he was none of those things. Sure, now he was certainly fit, but he got there from countless hours at the gym with a personal trainer. He had also started running but when it came to sports that involved a ball, a bat, a stick, or a team, Michael was completely out of his element, although he enjoyed being a spectator of sports.

"Oh, yeah, that's right. Nice to see you Beth. It's been a long time. You look great, by the way." Michael stumbled a little on his words, what was happening? Usually Michael was so smooth. Well, not today, he was nervous, uncomfortable, and attracted to Beth. It was like he was in high school all over again. Even his palms were sweaty.

What was wrong with him? He needed to focus. He was in Maine to help his parents get everything in order and to see his father, not get fixated on some bartender, even if she was Beth.

She was still in awe of how much he changed. She guessed he was just over six feet tall, and he was just so manly now. And while she like some muscles, she didn't want a gym-obsessed man. Michael was both tall and lean ... why was she even thinking about this? She had to focus, she had to manage the bar and come up with tomorrow's menu, she certainly had no time to think about a man who would surely be leaving town soon, let alone the man whose brother caused her sister's death. Despite her instant attraction to seeing him, it also caused her pain. It reminded her of that night.

The night of the state championships, her sister Jen let her boyfriend Jesse talk her out of driving her car home. They had both had too much to drink, and despite Beth and Michael's pleading, they left the party they were all at and left them behind. She guessed she should be thankful for that, but sometimes she wondered if she had been in the car if she could have done something to save them. Instead, she and Michael were drunk themselves, and had almost slept together.

It didn't matter. It was the past. She blinked back the tears she felt forming at the corners of her eyes. Had he said something, she thought, oh, yes, he had; she supposed she should respond instead of standing there, awkward and speechless.

"Um, well, thanks. You look great, too." She shouldn't have said that, was her attraction that obvious? She needed to get away and fast.

"Why don't I go check on your food." She stammered and walked away quickly.

Wow, Michael thought. Beth Adams. She was gorgeous. She had become more shapely than when they were teenagers; he could see how deeply blue her eyes were now that she wore contact lenses, and that red hair! He needed to calm down. He quickly drank his beer in an effort to ease his nerves. His palms were still sweaty. How could he get so nervous about a bartender? He had slept with countless bartenders and waitresses in New York, it was always the same: aspiring actress or model. He wanted more than a woman who was a bartender. Not to sound like a jerk but he couldn't get serious about someone who wasn't living their dream, no matter what it was. He wanted something more, he wanted a woman who was passionate, who loved what she did, and who was as focused as he had been. Then again, he was only going to be here for another couple of weeks.

Oh, hell, Beth probably got hit on all the time by creepy guys who came into the bar. Bartender or not, he didn't want to seem like a pig, especially with their history. Nothing had really happened other than a few frantic kisses, but much more could have. He would forget the advances he wished he could make for now.

He took another long swig of his beer as his oysters came out. Beth placed the plate in front of him and asked if he'd like another beer, to which he nodded amiably. When she came back with his beer, he had already had one of the oysters.

"Wow, these are great. If the rest of the food is like this, you'll be seeing a lot more of me while I am here."

He smiled and had another sip of his beer.

"Glad you like it." She should have ended it there but she just had to know, she loved hearing what people thought of her food.

"What's your favorite part?" She leaned in and asked.

He wanted to respond with, "all of you" as she leaned over the bar. Thank God she was behind the bar, otherwise she might know that all of her parts were his favorite and that he was having a very strong physical reaction to her. Instead, he tried to respond with a more respectable answer and secretly hoped she was asking a less respectable question in her own mind about him.

"I love the spinach fraîche but my favorite part is the potato crust. That hint of truffle, although subtle, is amazing. It really makes it upscale but not in the way that I feel silly ordering it at a bar, or rather, a tavern, if that makes sense. I feel like although these are special, I would love to taste it every day and wouldn't feel bad about it."

She got a little lost in his explanation, but it was exactly what she intended when she created it. She was unable to speak and realized she had been ignoring the other gentleman at the bar far too long. She just smiled, nodded, and headed over to the other end of the bar.

Wow, Michael thought. Beth Adams. At least there was one positive that had come from this terrible evening. Of course, he could never get involved with her, even if she was interested. His life was in New York and they had too much tragedy in their shared history, anyway. He began to work on his second beer and got lost in the game on the television. She came back with his steak and then eventually, as the other gentleman left the bar, she took a seat and began writing. He continued to watch the television and sip his beer.

He had to go home eventually, he just didn't want to. Home, he thought, where was home now? Maine never felt right before, New York didn't feel right now. What was he going to do with his life — hell, what was he going to do tomorrow? Maybe he should just leave and go back to New York now and face the music there. Hell, if he didn't figure something out soon, he might be bartending himself in a few months' time … or even sooner.

Beth was seated on the other end of the bar and looked over at Michael. Wow, he was certainly attractive. And there was still something soft about him, He had those sensitive eyes. He just always looked so understanding. She stopped herself. What was she thinking? He really didn't seem to be flirting anymore —which she hated to admit was a little disappointing. It had been a long time since Beth had a fling, let alone a relationship. Not really since she moved back here. Her brother Bob kept telling her to be more adventurous … but that just wasn't her. And what was it about this man? They had a history, a shared experience — but not exactly a pleasant one that connected them. But there was something more to it than that. Anyway, it didn't matter. Even if she could get beyond the memories of Jenny he dredged up and their own past, he said he'd only be here a few weeks. Also, who could take off a few weeks these days…and why come here? Even though it was a beautiful little town, she never expected to be living here as an adult.

She snuck another look at him. It was startling how much someone could change in thirteen years. She had also changed, but she didn't feel like it was nearly as dramatic. His blue polo shirt stretched over his taut muscles and tight stomach. It looked like he spent a lot of time in the gym, but he wasn't ultra muscular and didn't have the look of a "meathead." He looked lean and fit. She liked that. He was also clean-cut. And although the glasses hid his handsome face somewhat, she had to admit they made him look hot.

She always kind of liked nerdy guys — which was why she was attracted to him in high school, instead of his brother, whom everyone worshipped. She had never really liked Jesse. And she liked him even less after that night … the night her sister died. She guessed it was because he had seemed privileged and worshipped. She knew Michael came from the same family but she had felt differently about him; he was an outsider looking in, just like she had been. Sure, she hung out with the cool kids but it was only because she played basketball. She did that so she could get a scholarship, which she did. But she always felt out of place. Maybe it was because she was poor, maybe it was because she was taller than everyone and a "Ginger." Ginger was her nickname in high school, not one that she particularly enjoyed but it beat carrot top. Jesse Malone and his crew could be mean about it, despite his relationship with her sister. What made Michael any different?

She had to remind herself that he hadn't exactly been an insider in high school, either. He was always a solitary figure and was always busy working at the market. She wondered what he was doing now, and again, why he was in town? Why now?

At least he had a good appreciation for food, she thought. She looked over and watched him eat his steak; he really looked like he was enjoying it. She went back to work on her menu for the next day. Then she looked over at Michael again. He had pushed his plate to the side and was just staring at his beer. She looked at the clock; it was already ten thirty. She hurriedly moved from her seat and got behind the bar. It was just the two of them in there.

"So, how was the steak?" she asked.

Michael had been deep in thought, but at the sound of her voice, he came to and said, "Oh, the steak was great, thank you. I really enjoyed it."

He looked around the bar, which was empty. What had he been doing all this time? He was off in space, thinking about what he was going to do for his family. Could he even help them after what his dad had said? He knew he had to. He also thought about Beth and how her black pencil skirt fit so snugly against her hips, and her white collared shirt really emphasized her long, lovely neck. And those eyes, that face, and her hair—.

"Would you like anything else?" she asked.

He came back to earth. He knew the bar closed at

eleven on Mondays, so she probably wanted to get home to her boyfriend or husband. For some reason, the idea of her with another man waiting for her at home annoyed Michael. Not that he thought he had any right to feel that way.

"A glass of water and the check would be great."

He should be good to drive, but after what had happened to Jesse, he was always extra cautious about drinking and driving. Living in New York he rarely had to worry about it, but whenever he traveled, he would always be mindful. Some people thought he wasn't as fun as he could be because of it, but it mattered to him.

She came back with the glass of water and Michael felt like he had worked up a little courage.

She handed it to him and he said, "Thank you. I hope you don't mind, is it okay if I just sit here and drink this for a little while before I drive? I know you probably want to get back to your boyfriend or husband, so if it's a problem I can just go sit in my car for a bit."

Beth was so nervous all of a sudden. Husband or boyfriend? Was he hitting on her or just being polite? He didn't seem to show interest before, but asking about whether she was attached was definitely a sign of interest. She felt her body grow warm and she felt what she always referred to as the body blush coming on. God, this was embarrassing.

"Oh, no, no husband or boyfriend to rush home to. I'm very single ... I mean, stay as long as you like. I won't be closing things out for another hour before I head home." She stammered and blushed a deep red. Her face nearly matched her hair. She was embarrassed.

'I'm very single'? Who says that! She could just

71

kick herself.

He could tell she was embarrassed, but it made her more endearing, he thought. "Thank you," he said, as he smiled sadly.

He was a mess, maybe if things could have been different, a woman like Beth would come home to him at night. But he had made choices that put him where he was today. Single, alienated from his family, and soon to be jobless. He chuckled to himself; he was also very single. It made him wonder what her story was. He stared down at his water, not knowing what he was going to do next.

He stayed just sitting there for another half hour. She busied herself with closing the books and cleaning the bar, things she assumed her regular bar staff would be doing. It was kind of nice: the calm of it all, but all the customer interaction was not her favorite thing in the world. Although, if the customers were all like Michael, she decided it might not be too bad.

Michael got up and walked over to the end of the bar to say goodnight to Beth. He brought over his glass, setting it down on the bar, and said to her, "Thanks so much for everything tonight. Here's my glass and the check. Thanks again, I hope to see you soon." Then he smiled and left.

Beth stared after him. Michael seemed like a pleasant enough guy, handsome, just the right amount of nerdy, but she could just tell something was missing. He seemed deeply sad.

Beth wondered. It had been a long time since she felt an attraction like this and it had certainly been a long time since her last date. Maybe — oh, forget it, she thought. She had to focus on her menus. After all, it was tourist season and you never knew when a food critic might stop by. She needed to focus. No out-of-towners for her, especially not ones with history ... no matter how sexy.

CHAPTER SIX

Beth came to work the next morning feeling a little distracted. Seeing Michael the night before had caused a flood of memories for her, and not all of them were pleasant. High school had been tough; being in the 'in crowd' was costly. And for Beth, being 'in' was really not being in. Being on the basketball team meant she got invited to all the parties and was included in things she otherwise might not have been, but she always felt out of place. Basically, her height had been both a blessing and burden in high school. Being able to play basketball was the obvious blessing; the burden really was the taunting. And guys like Michael's brother Jesse, and his football goons, were the ones who made life just a little more difficult. That eased up once her sister and Jesse started dating. But Beth never understood what Jenny saw in him.

Things had changed a lot since high school. Beth didn't always know she wanted to be a chef. In fact, she had tried to convince herself to become a doctor, but after her parents had passed away, she picked up cooking with her grandmother. Her older sister was too busy out with the 'in crowd' but Beth stuck around and helped out. As her grandmother continued to age, Beth began taking over the cooking at home. Her grandmother was always an excellent cook. It was one of the reasons Beth loved the holidays so much. Her grandmother and she spent many Friday nights and Sundays in the kitchen just baking and experimenting with new recipes. And when Beth had decided she wanted to go to culinary school instead of studying medicine or something 'practical,' her grandmother had supported her through it.

Fortunately, the university Beth attended in Rhode Island had not only an excellent culinary program, but it also had a women's basketball team. When she graduated, she managed to get out and work at some of the top restaurants in both Providence and Boston, but a few years ago she finally decided she wanted more. She wanted something of her own and she wanted to put down roots somewhere. Boston was too expensive and Providence had never felt like home.

Beth came back to Gray Harbor before her youngest sibling headed off to college. A grand old home near the Gray Harbor Lighthouse had been in bad repair and eventually made it to the auction block. Beth had saved some money and decided to bid on it. Her grandmother pitched in, too.

The original property also had a small guesthouse, which Beth now made her home. She lived with her little sister Lisa and with her grandmother, and they had frequent visits from her brother, Bob. After extensive renovations, three years ago the buildings were completed. Now the Warren Inn and Tavern, named for the former homeowners, had become a hit not only with tourists but also with locals. Beth had a restaurant that served dinner each night and did a special brunch on Sundays for the after-church crowd.

The tavern offered a more limited selection than the Inn's restaurant but it became a popular place for locals to have burgers and beers and meet out-of-towners while watching a ball game. She looked around and smiled at what was around her now. She could hardly believe it. When she was a child, her family had struggled to put any food on the table and now here she was, feeding others oysters, caviar, Angus beef, and lobster. Thinking of where she had come from, and where she was now, made her smile. What made her even happier was that her little sister Lisa had decided to follow in her footsteps to become a chef. In fact, Lisa would be Beth's Sous Chef this summer. It took a little soul searching for Lisa to set her mind on the culinary arts, but Beth was excited that she had and that made Beth even prouder that Lisa was now attending the prestigious Johnson and Whales after making some tough decisions.

Beth went to the kitchen and took a quick inventory of what they had and what they would need before Lisa came in. There was a bicycle tour group arriving tomorrow and she wanted to be ready for them. Lisa had stumbled upon their biking/culinary tours online and reached out to them. If things went well this weekend, the Inn would host them four times this summer, as well as accommodate them for some fall trips. This would really help boost the Inn's business and help make it a tourist destination!

She was happy about all the success she had achieved but she felt like some things were passing her by in life. She was always so busy and dating was tough. She was always cooking on weekends and her restaurant was one of the hottest date spots in town. It was always awkward for someone to bring her there and then learn she was the owner. Not a big deal to her, but often men were uncomfortable with her success, and with the knowledge that there was no chance she'd pick up and leave for them. The only men she seemed to meet who didn't care about that weren't exactly what she was looking for. She wanted someone who lived a life beyond Gray Harbor. Gray Harbor was a great place, but for Beth it had taken leaving for her to realize just how great. Speaking of leaving, she was wondering where Michael was off to and what he had been up to for all these years.

***

The next morning, she couldn't help herself. When she got to the Inn, she called her brother Bob, who was undoubtedly her best friend and closest confidant.

"Hey Beth! Do you have any idea what time it is?" said Bob.

"Oh, come on, Bobby, it's only seven," said Beth.

"Okay, okay. So what's up?"

"Michael Malone came in last night ... I barely recognized him."

"Mmmhmm. Now I'm awake. Do tell?" said Bob.

"Not much to tell. Good taste in food, looks good in glasses." She began to feel oddly turned on just

77

thinking about him.

"I heard Mr. Malone is sick, I bet that's why he's back in town," said Bob.

How terrible, thought Beth. That explained Michael's sullen demeanor at the bar last night, she thought.

"What exactly does he do that he could take leave like this?" asked Beth.

"Well, apparently he's some big time executive in New York. But why are you so interested, anyway? Wait a second. You have the hots for him!"

"NO! No, I do not. He's not someone I'd ever be involved with. I mean, for one he's just passing through, two, he's not even interested, and three, the Malones aren't exactly my favorite people," said Beth, trying to convince herself.

"Oh, please! Excuses. You can't blame the guy for his brother's actions. And what's wrong with a little fling here and there? You could stand to get laid!"

"Bob!" said Beth in shock.

"What! Oh, come on, don't tell me you weren't thinking it, too!"

She didn't want to admit it but she *was* thinking it. Michael was just passing through, not someone who she should get involved with. Not that he had indicated any strong interest anyway. Even Bob admitted that Michael was quite handsome. But a handsome face doesn't always lead to a relationship ... it usually leads to heartache. After she and Bob hung up, Beth sat there in the kitchen, thinking about the night before. She was so deep in thought she didn't even notice her sister Lisa walk in.

"Hello, McFly, earth to Beth," Lisa said loudly,

referencing one of Beth's favorite old movies from the eighties.

Beth snapped out of it. "Oh, hey there, sis! You ready to discuss the menu for the week?"

"Totally!" Lisa said.

Beth smiled. She loved the twenty-four-year-old's enthusiasm. Beth felt like having Lisa around just energized her, and it would certainly take her mind off Michael. She would be sad to see Lisa go back to school again in the fall. But was hoping that after graduating, Lisa would consider being Beth's partner in the business. Lisa had started off pursuing business but much like Beth decided her true path was to cook and was back in school.

"So, here's what I am thinking; six of the cyclists are vegetarians, so a zucchini lentil pie could be an option. It would be like shepherd's pie but vegetarian and extra delicious, and I was thinking for sides we can do grilled asparagus, herb salad, and that delicious truffle vinaigrette you make. What do you think?"

Beth smiled. "That sounds amazing. Let's test it out this morning, and if they like it, let's add it to the fall/winter menu. It's a little hearty but I think that with all their biking, they'll work up an appetite for it."

Lisa looked like she was slightly disappointed but perked up and said," I also thought of something lighter that I think could be a great appetizer or even an entree: bay scallops, frisée, grapefruit, and I'm thinking we add sherry? I read up on that but I've never really had sherry, so I'm not sure?"

Beth exclaimed, "Now, that's a great idea! I like it, let's add that to the overall menu for the week, as well. I was also thinking some halibut would be good. We can herb baste it and then make a little crab and spinach ravioli and add a lobster cream on that."

Lisa nodded with enthusiasm. It wasn't often that someone so young in their culinary career got to come up with new menu items like she did at the Warren. "Great, well, why don't you get started on the prep and I'll head over to Malone's Market and see if they have enough for us."

"I can go to Malone's if you like, Beth?" Lisa offered.

"No, that's all right. I really want you to get started on the scallop recipe and the lentil pie. Also, make sure the staff is ready for tonight's menu, we'll use the one I wrote up last night for our specials," said Beth.

She noticed her sister's disappointment and wondered what was at Malone's Market that was of interest to her. Maybe it was just the thrill of fresh ingredients. That's always what did it for Beth. She smiled and headed out of the kitchen and into her office. She was going to make a list and head to Malone's for some of the supplies she needed. She loved Malone's for her seafood, she just wished they would finish up so she wouldn't have to go across town to Cinzano's Market. As a chain, Cinzano's didn't have access to all of the local fishermen like Malone's did. But she had to admit if it weren't for the fish, she probably wouldn't do business with Malone's, not with how things there were lately.

***

Michael was back at Malone's Market by six that morning. He decided that whether his father liked it or not, he was going to help the family any way he could.

By noon, he had everything sorted and ready for review and eventually to be color-coded and filed. Doing this was cathartic and it helped him take two things off his mind: his father and Beth. Even though he and Beth didn't interact for a long period of time last night, and despite the fact she wasn't exactly his "type," he couldn't fight his attraction for her, and he didn't really know what he wanted to do about that.

So for the time being, his plan was to ignore those feelings and focus on the tasks at hand. He was ready to finally get to the bottom of the family's troubles and get them a little more organized, and he didn't want to stray from that mission. He had around two and half weeks left here and then it was back to his own trouble. It's funny, it was only Tuesday but it felt like he had been here forever. Not once since he'd been here had he received a call or even an email from work. And although he was on vacation, his office wasn't exactly the kind of place that respected people's personal time or vacation schedules. You had to be all in all the time … unless you were out. And by out, Michael thought, he meant finished with the company, as in fired, or, worse yet, demoted. That was something Michael couldn't accept. Michael pushed those thoughts out of his mind and he went to the first stack, bills. He figured he'd get that started and make some spreadsheets and then get them organized and filed away.

Just as he was looking up from the computer, he noticed Annie had popped in. Her long brown hair was pulled back and her blue eyes looked serious. She was wearing her usual Malone's Market t-shirt and jeans.

"Hey, little brother, how goes it?" said Annie.

Michael knew she wanted to talk about their

father, but he wasn't really in the mood. So he responded and said, "Going all right, I'm just about to tackle the bills."

She nodded, sensing that it wasn't up for discussion, and asked, "What time did you get in? I drove up a little before eight and your car was already here? What are you trying to do — make me look bad?" she smiled.

"No, I just wanted to get an early start and tackle some of the more tedious work before anything more fun could pop up."

By fun, he meant stressful. Annie grasped his meaning and smiled again.

"So, Mom isn't here today. She went to run some errands and spend a little extra time with Dad. Any chance we can get some lunch and then maybe you can help me out on the floor today? Tuesday can sometimes be a busy day here and I need all the help I can get."

Michael looked down at his dress khakis and his button-down shirt and expensive Italian loafers. Not exactly appropriate for being a fish-monger for the day. Annie noticed that he was looking down at his outfit.

She rolled her eyes. "Relax, Mr. Fancy Pants, I just want you to ring people up, maybe work the cheese counter? Think you can handle that?"

"Aye Aye, Captain," Michael said sarcastically, while giving Annie a military salute. He smiled at her visible annoyance.

"All right, all right, let's get some food. I brought you a sandwich because I figured you wouldn't have one. I made the kids PB and J today so I made us some too."

Michael realized in the four days he had been back he had not yet seen all of the kids or Tom. "How are the kids? And Tom? Maybe I could, I don't know, come over one night and play. Or better yet, why don't I babysit one night so you and Tom can have a night out? "

Annie looked stunned. " Are you kidding?"

Michael was surprised she would be so surprised, but then realized he hadn't really taken an active interest, aside from sending the kids gifts and cards ... and his secretary took care of all that.

"Yeah, I'm serious. I'd like to hang out with my nephews and after doing this initial work here in the office, I'm realizing how hard you've been working. You deserve a night off. And you know, the Warren Inn's tavern has great food, you should check it out."

"Do they? I've been meaning to go. Beth and her sister Lisa come here all the time to buy their seafood and she's been telling me to come in. Thank god they still come here. She's one of our biggest customers."

"Beth Adams?" Michael was confused, was Annie talking about the same Beth?

"Yeah, Beth, you remember her. The tall redhead. Her sister dated Jesse? She's the owner of the Warren Inn and Tavern and also the chef."

Michael still wasn't able to process all of this.

"Didn't you go there last night? Maybe she wasn't there. Beth is amazing and she insists on supporting the local businesses. Thank god for that, she's our most consistent revenue. Another reason I could use your help is that she's going to be keeping me pretty busy today. She's doing these new culinary bike tours and offers them special menus each time, which is great for us, 'cause she develops the menus on the fly and likes to keep it very local. Very Maine, you know?"

Michael couldn't believe his ears. Beth Adams was the chef and owner of the whole inn! He had to admit it was really well done and quite cosmopolitan for Gray Harbor, and the culinary bike tours ... what a brilliant idea. Gray Harbor was, after all, quite beautiful for that sort of thing. He had her all wrong. Not that it mattered what she did for a living really. It didn't change anything; he still couldn't get into anything with her. He was leaving soon. But he supposed there was no harm in a little flirting or even making friends. After all, two and half weeks was a long time.

She was going to be here today. Suddenly being out on the floor today didn't sound so bad. He perked up.

"All right, I'll be out on the floor. But let's eat lunch; I'm starving all of a sudden. I'll pick up on the bills tonight."

Annie and Michael headed over to Annie's office and had some peanut butter and jelly sandwiches and sodas. Michael couldn't help thinking it would be great if there were more places to get lunch around here. It might be nice to have a food stand or even an eatery here at Malone's. Something to think about. Before he suggested any other new ideas, though, he figured he should get a better handle on the business and the current situation.

Annie and Michael made small talk as they ate and decided that Michael would babysit the next night while she and Tom finally had a night to themselves to do anything, maybe even just go out for a movie or a drink at the Tavern. Michael was glad he made someone in his family happy by being there. They finished up and Annie took Michael downstairs and got him ready for his afternoon shift as cashier.

CHAPTER SEVEN

Beth pulled up to Malone's Market. Although she liked the new space, she had to admit she missed the smaller market it once was. Of course she would never tell Annie that, given all the work she and her family had put into the place.

Over the past three years, she had really come to respect Annie. Beth believed in small business, but frankly, she was worried for the Malones. With Cinzano's cornering the specialty food market in Gray Harbor, it might be hard for Malone's to make a comeback — but again, Malone's was Maine.

As Beth got out of the car, she checked her hair and makeup. She didn't usually care what she looked like to meet Annie, but she couldn't help thinking maybe she'd run into Michael. She was slightly embarrassed that she might meet him wearing her chef's jacket and checkered chef pants and clogs, but she had to live with it. And besides, he didn't exactly seem like the kind of guy who would work at the fish market. Maybe he wouldn't be there at all and she was stressing out for nothing. She knew he did in high school but, well, Beth didn't really know what to expect. And frankly, she didn't know why seeing him again was taking up so much space in her brain. She locked her car and headed for the entrance.

She walked through the market area and decided she'd look to see if she could find grapefruit for the scallops. She found a few that were acceptable and placed them in her basket. She then found some frisée and few other items. She didn't usually buy produce here, but since this was for a special menu and it was "on the fly," she figured why not.

She had made her way down the aisles and was reading a package of soba noodles, lost in thought about making the idea of making some pickled lotus root, and tuna steak with soba, when she felt someone behind her.

"Can I help you find anything?" Michael said with a smile.

Beth spun around and was a bit speechless. He wasn't wearing his glasses and today he wore a white dress shirt, which was open just enough to see his tanned skin and just a tiny sprinkling of hair. He had on Italian leather loafers and khaki dress slacks, flat front, thank god, she noted. She hated men who wore pleated pants. He certainly didn't look like a fishmonger, but he strangely resembled some of her more Wall Street guests at the Inn, who she didn't always love—he looked very "Flatlander". He looked like a tourist. Well, whatever, she thought, he did he look good today.

She pondered his question and asked, "Can you help me with anything ... wait, do you work here now, Michael?" She asked, feeling a little self-conscious.

Michael wondered if it really mattered whether he worked here or not. Beth didn't strike him as a woman who really cared whether he was a doctor, lawyer, or bag boy. But then again, he had reacted similarly about her.

"Well, I am working here today." He smiled. "I'm just here helping out for a few weeks while I'm on vacation."

That was nice, she thought. And also surprising, from the little she did know about Michael and his relationship with his family. Bob had told her that Michael never came to visit and that he and his father were not on the best of terms. She also remembered that in high school, he had been living under Jesse's shadow. She didn't want to pry but she assumed if he was here for a while, then his father must not be doing so great. She and Annie hadn't had a heart-to-heart recently. They weren't exactly the best of friends but they did see each other every Tuesday during her shopping excursions.

Michael looked down at her basket and said, "So, are you shopping for yourself today?"

"Oh, no, I'm actually shopping for the Warren Inn today. I'm planning this week's menu and doing all the shopping for our specials."

He nodded. "That explains the chef's outfit. I had no idea you were both an accomplished chef and bartender." He smiled.

"Ahh, yes that. I'm probably the world's worst bartender. I was just covering for a staff member who called in sick. Actually, I'm the owner and head chef of the inn," she paused adding, "and the occasional bartender, waitress ... valet parking attendant."

What the hell was she doing, she thought to herself. This man is here helping his family because his father is sick and she was making a pass at him. And he clearly lived so far away that he couldn't possibly want anything more than a fling. Now, there was a thought: a fling. She could feel herself blushing, maybe he wouldn't notice.

He chuckled at her response and said, "A woman of many talents."

"Now, my capabilities are not nearly as impressive but do you need anything I can help you with today, selecting a cheese, fish? Or perhaps—"

Michael was cut off by Annie, "Beth! So glad you're here. Is my baby brother bothering you?!"

Now it was Michael's turn to blush.

"I'm sorry, did I interrupt something?" Annie asked, clearly confused.

Beth responded with, "No, no not at all. Michael was just helping me find a few things," she said, as she held up her soba noodles.

"Ok, well great then! Well, do I have things to show you today," she said, as she hooked Beth's arm under her own and steered her away. Beth looked over her shoulder back at Michael. He was looking back at her and smiled, shrugging his shoulders at his sister. Beth had siblings, too, and felt she completely understood. In a span of two seconds they had silently communicated. And unless Beth was completely dense, she thought they communicated a mutual interest and a "let's pick up on this later" look. Or, at least, she was hoping that's what that was. She turned her head and tried to focus on what Annie was saying — Annie was speaking a mile a minute.

"–So, I was also thinking that you need to see the halibut but also these anchovies. I was watching the food network just the other day and I said to Tom, look at these amazing Caesar club sandwiches. It was the barefoot ladies show, you know, and it would just be perfect at the tavern ..."

Michael stood watching them and eventually Annie's banter faded away. He never thought he'd say this, but a beautiful woman all covered up was actually pretty hot. Granted, she was wearing a baggie chef's jacket and those little checked chef's pants ... but there was just something about the way she looked, especially with all that fiery red hair pinned back. He wished he could do something about what he was feeling, but then again, a woman like Beth was probably looking to settle down. He wanted those things, too, but he lived in New York and she lived all the way here in Maine.

And what did he really know about her, anyway? Sure, she was attractive, and no doubt talented, but what else did Michael really know? Was it really worth it to be spinning his wheels about this woman whom he had exchanged nothing more than a few flirtatious words and glances with? All he knew now was that he wasn't thinking straight and he had another few hours of "on the floor" work and then a night of paperwork. And then a day of more Malone's Market and home repairs.

Michael was in a daze the rest of day. He bagged groceries, rang customers up, mopped spills, and chatted with customers. He was exhausted. His day job was nothing like this. Sure he worked hard, but he wasn't on his feet all day. He tried to be extra helpful wherever possible and whenever he had no customers, he was cleaning or trying to stay busy and forget about not only Beth, but his father and his family's troubles. As far as he could see, there was a loyal customer base here at Malone's Market, but they weren't doing much to retain them. And these renovations were not well-planned.

Time had flown and before he knew it, it was seven thirty and Michael had barely seen Annie since she and Beth had left him in the aisles earlier that day.

Annie must have read his mind because at that moment, she finally appeared. "Hey, slacker, what have you been doing all day?" She smiled.

Annie, always making jokes at Michael's expense. After they filled each other in on the details of the day, Annie walked Michael through the closing process. Cashing out the registers, checking the slips, noting the returns, listing what would need to be restocked, getting the bank deposits ready, and managing the staff for cleanup. At the end of it all, Annie called Tom to let him know she'd be staying late. Annie had decided that maybe tackling the paperwork together would go faster. They sat down in their father's office and started getting down to the business at hand.

"What the! How is this even possible, Michael?" she exclaimed after two hours of going through the bills and looking at the revenue spreadsheet Michael had been working on. They were losing money every day they were open. Annie looked at Michael in disbelief.

"How, how could he let this happen to the market ... to, to all of us," Annie stuttered. She looked as if she was near tears.

"Okay, Annie, calm down. I think it's pretty

simple. I think Dad miscalculated and may have gotten a little overconfident. I think he figured with the improvements, profits would just go up. But he didn't account for all of the renovation costs, permit costs, and lost business due to all of this. He did no marketing and no retention work," said Michael matter-of-factly.

"Okay, Mikey. Just hang on, none of this mumbo jumbo business school crap. What do we do now?"

Michael tried to think rationally ... basically his family was $374,000 in the hole ... which was a hell of a lot of money for anyone. Taxes would be higher with all the improvements and they needed some serious work done to the place now. Along with marketing costs, new inventory, and maybe even that food stand ... basically they needed at least $500,000 to get them out of this. That was a lot. Michael could swing it, but he knew his dad wouldn't go for it.

Annie was looking at him, waiting for an answer.

"Well?" she asked. "Now what?"

"We need five hundred thousand."

"*What?* Oh, my God, I don't even know what to say to that. Oh, my God. Do you think, do you think he knows?"

Michael couldn't see how his father wouldn't know, but he didn't want to say so. "I don't know, Annie, he might not. This place was a mess till the other day and it's not that obvious. A miscalculation here and there and ..." He stopped himself.

"I don't know, Annie, but it's not good. I think we need to tell Mom and then figure out what to do from there. I can cover some of this and get us through, but I think that would really upset Dad."

Annie nodded; she knew it was true. "You're right, we need to talk to Mom. But I want to know something, Michael. Do you think that even if we figure out a way to cover the money that the business could succeed? I'm starting to worry. I just, I just have invested so much time here, and with Tom not knowing what's next with the Navy and the kids ..."

"It's going to be okay; we'll figure something out, Annie. I think I can help if Mom and Dad will let me. And I want to help. I really do."

And Michael meant it. He really did. He didn't know what was going on here, but he knew he could make a difference. And after the year he'd been having in New York, that was a really great feeling. And being able to make a difference and have it help his family instead of making a bunch of rich people richer seemed right. He still didn't want to work at Malone's Market, he thought to himself. Well, maybe that wasn't really true anymore. Maybe he did. The thought shocked him. But he didn't want to unless he and his father could resolve their issues. Until then, he would just do what he could for the next two and a half weeks. He couldn't believe it was already Tuesday, yet he also couldn't believe it was only Tuesday. So much had happened since he arrived this past weekend.

"So, what are you going to do with the rest of your night, Mikey?" asked Annie, "'cause I could sure use a drink."

Michael smiled, it had been a while since Annie and he had drinks together. Not since her last trip to New York to visit him.

"Let's do it."

They closed down the computer, hit the lights,

and headed to the parking lot.

"I'll drive," offered Michael.

"Nah, I will. Tom will be really annoyed if I not only came home late but drunk on top of that. We can leave your car here. I'll pick you up on my way in tomorrow, good deal?"

He nodded and with that they walked to her car and got in.

"Hey, wait, where are we going to go, doesn't every place close at like eleven?"

"Eleven? Hell, no. Well, Mondays the Tavern closes early but from Tuesday on they're open till one and yeah, we're going there. It really is the only game in town if you want a nice glass a wine. Which is what I'm feeling like right now."

Annie put the keys in the ignition, pulled out of the parking lot, and headed for the Warren Inn. Even though Michael was both emotionally and physically exhausted, he found himself perking up. He wondered if the bartender from last night was out sick again ... he hoped so. At the thought, he smiled to himself.

CHAPTER EIGHT

"So, what can I get you two?" said the bartender from behind the bar.

"Hey, Michael, right?"

"Yeah! Bob? From McAllister's?"

"The one and only! And who is the gorgeous young lady with you, you cradle robber?" Bob smiled at Annie.

"Bob, this is my sister Annie."

"Oh, of course I know Annie! My sister Beth just loves you, talks about you all the time. So, what can I get you?"

Annie smiled and looked at the chalkboard and said, "I'll have the Pinot Noir."

"Make that two," Michael added with a smile.

"Coming right up!"

"Wow," said Annie. "I haven't seen Bob in ages. He is some looker, look at all those muscles."

Michael looked over at Bob. No doubt he did have a lot of muscles under that tight black Armani t-shirt and dark, slim-fit jeans. He was sporting a very different look than he had at McAllister's. Bob had style, that was for sure. And he had the same sparkle in his eyes as Beth.

"Annie, you're a married woman," said Michael

with a humorous look on his face.

"Well, I'm not dead yet. Its good genes, you know. Don't think I didn't notice you drooling over his sister today."

Before Michael could respond, Bob was back with their drinks.

"Here you go, guys! Oh, and Annie, just so you know, Beth gets off work at eleven thirty so you may catch her then, if you like. I'm sure she would love to see you again today." With that, he winked and walked off to help the next guest.

The bar was a little more crowded this evening than last night, Michael observed. Probably because there was a game on the television, but Michael couldn't even focus on that. What Annie had said totally threw him off.

"What do you mean, I was drooling?" asked Michael.

Annie took a sip of her wine and waved her hand, "Oh, please, neither of you were hiding it well. It's clear you're both attracted to each other, and all I have to say is jump on that! You couldn't find a better person than Beth. She's gorgeous, smart, successful, and a total sweetheart."

And she was incredibly sexy, too, Michael thought.

"Oh, come on, I don't need anyone now, I'm fine," said Michael unconvincingly, as he took a sip of his wine.

"Okay, so little brother, what's the deal? Something is up, I know it. Usually whenever I see you you're glued to your phone. But I haven't even seen you look at that thing once. You haven't obsessively checked the markets on your iPad. And not once, not once, have I heard you talk about your stupid portfolio. What gives?"

Wow, so was that what he was like. She made him sound like a money-obsessed workaholic. The more he pondered it, it did seem that way. But the money didn't matter so much; he liked being right about the numbers and the "more right" he was, the bigger payoff. She was right, he hadn't checked the markets or seriously tried to reach the office.

Before he had time to think about it, the words came out of his mouth. "I want to quit my job, Annie. I want to quit my job and come back here. Maybe I'll help at the market, maybe I'll open up a small shop of my own. I'm just not happy in New York anymore."

Wow, he had said it. He really said it, and he had meant it.

Annie almost dropped her glass of wine. "Wait, wait. You want to quit your job and come back here? Here to the place you ran away from?" She was now smirking sarcastically.

Michael sighed. "Point taken."

Annie suddenly got serious, "I would love that, Michael. I think we all would." She put her hand over his. "Even Dad."

Michael didn't know about that; he didn't even know why he had said what he did.

"So, have you quit yet? Is that why you could be here for so long?"

Michael took another sip of his wine, actually a gulp, and then began his story. He had not talked to anyone about this and it felt good. He explained what was going on with the partners of the fund and that they were trying to push him out by pinning some bad trades on him. He had made enough money to get out, he just didn't know if he should quit with his pride intact, or wait for the huge payoff.

Annie finished off the last of her wine and said, "Okay, the next drink is on me, Mikey, and it's gonna be a strong one. This sounds like a terrible situation." She flagged Bob down and asked him for a glass of water for herself and a scotch for Michael.

"If it were me, I'd go out in a blaze of glory and march my ass over there and tell them to go take their money and stuff it, you know where. I mean, it's not exactly like you're broke, right?"

"No, not at all. I mean, I could just sell my place in the city and easily get a little house here and start my own thing and still manage to help out the market and be all right."

"Well, then …" She paused as Bob brought over their drinks. She handed Michael his and clinked their glasses. "Cheers to you then, little bro. Tell those jerks to go you-know-where!"

Annie looked down at her watch as Michael was downing his drink.

"Mikey, it's already eleven thirty. Tom isn't gonna like this, are you still on to babysit tomorrow? Could you do it till late night?"

"Yeah, of course. Speaking of late night, is there a cab I could get from here?"

Annie suddenly had a devilish look in her eye. "Sure, I'll make sure you have a ride. I'll be right back." And with that, Annie had walked away.

Michael turned to see where she was going and then he saw that she had walked right up to Beth and pointed in his direction. Michael tried to make out what they were saying but his lip-reading skills were seriously lacking. He looked at Beth; she looked amazing. She had changed her clothes since earlier that day and was now wearing skinny jeans, strappy sandals, and a light blue fitted oxford shirt with the sleeves rolled up. Her hair was down and if he wasn't mistaken, her eyes sparkled with some mischievousness, as she looked his way. He smiled and nodded in her direction.

Annie led Beth over to where Michael was standing.

"Hey, Mikey, good news. I asked Beth about getting you a cab and she offered to make sure you got home all right."

Beth smiled at him.

"I'll get the check, Michael," Annie said, and she leaned over and whispered, "Just tell me where to pick you up in the morning." She winked at him and waved Bob over.

"Don't worry about it, I got it, Annie. I'll see you tomorrow morning."

Bob walked over as Annie was heading out. "Hey, sis! How am I doing tonight? Look at all these happy customers!"

Beth smiled at her little brother.

"Looking good, Bob. Can you get me a glass of my favorite Chardonnay?"

"You got it sis, and for you, Michael?"

"I'll just have another of the same, thanks Bob." Michael smiled as he raised his glass at Bob.

Beth grabbed the bar stool next to Michael and said, "Twice in one day Michael, I'm beginning to think you're following me." She smiled flirtatiously.

Michael smiled at her and thought, why argue with her.

"You're right, I am following you. Glad you don't seem to mind," he said, as he scooted slightly closer.

Bob came by with their drinks and quickly walked away, giving his sister a knowing glance.

"So, Michael, what have you been up to since you last dropped rubber bands on our Bunsen burners in high school?"

Michael laughed out loud. He had forgotten all about that.

While working in the lab one day, Michael accidentally dropped a rubber band on one of the burners and it had smelled absolutely awful. Michael wasn't the best of lab partners. He was a little uncoordinated but Beth always took it in stride.

"I don't know why you didn't just ask for a new partner, I was the absolute worst in chemistry."

Hmm, chemistry, she thought as she sipped her chardonnay.

"But forget about me, I haven't done anything too exciting. I'd love to hear all about you and what you've been up to since I saw you last?"

"Well, I've been cooking since this afternoon, but aside from that, not much," she said with a twinkle in her eyes.

"Oh, so I see, that's how it's going to be. I, unlike you, am willing to share," he said jokingly.

He told her about moving to New York for his undergrad. How he worked as a commodities trader for a few years, got his MBA, and now managed a hedge fund.

"I knew it," she said. "I had you pegged as a

finance guy at first glance but then, and don't take offense to this, but after talking to you I didn't think you seemed to be a big enough jerk to do that for a living. I always thought you'd become a writer or something."

For the second time tonight, he couldn't believe he was saying this. "I'm actually thinking of leaving my job and moving a little closer to home. I don't have all the details worked out, but I want to be around for my family more than I have been."

She looked a little surprised.

He added, "And well ... I wasn't a big enough jerk to be able to do finance forever. So it's time to move on."

Beth was completely shocked. In high school, all Michael had wanted was to get out of Maine as quickly as possible — and now he wanted to come back?

"Well Michael, I think you'll find Maine has lots to offer, that maybe you didn't notice before," Beth's cheeks quickly colored.

Michael had finished up his drink and before he could even think to ask for another, Beth flagged her brother down and he was back with fresh drinks and water before Michael could think of what to say next.

"Thank you, Bob." He nodded to Bob and clinked glasses with Beth. With the combination of the wine and the scotches he had been drinking he was starting to feel quite tipsy.

"So, Beth, what about you? I heard you had a scholarship playing basketball after high school?"

Beth told him all about how cooking was her first love when she was a child. She talked about her experiences studying culinary arts, about cooking in

Boston. She also told him how she got tired of the big city rat race and that she could relate to him in that way.

He nodded enthusiastically as she continued to tell him about how she came to own the Warren Inn and how it had become a real family business. Bob had done the decorating, Lisa worked in the kitchen, and even her grandmother pitched in at the reception desk from time to time. She felt like she had been rambling, but Michael was listening intently and actually looked interested in what she was saying. They talked some more about what each of them had been up to and about how much Gray Harbor had changed since they were kids.

She looked at Michael now. He was smiling and his knees were touching hers. She smiled back at him and looked down at her hands and then looked around the room for the first time in two hours. Again, they were the last ones there except for her brother. Michael noticed her looking around the bar and then took a look himself.

"Wow, looks like we closed this place down," Michael said, as he grabbed both her hands with his.

"I'm really glad we had a chance to talk tonight. I haven't had such a good time with someone in a very long time," said Michael, still looking at her intently.

Her skin tingled and she had this overwhelming urge to lean over and kiss him but she didn't want to risk breaking contact.

Bob walked over at that moment and said, "Hey, Beth and Michael. I need close up here. Michael, can I get you your check?"

Beth was about to object but then Michael caught

her eye.

"I'd like to get Beth's drinks as well, if that's ok," Michael reached into his wallet and pulled out his credit card and handed it to Bob. "I mean, if you don't mind, Beth."

How could she mind, she thought. It felt like a date and it was strange. Usually, when men met her here, they never asked for the check or thought to make the gesture since she was the owner. Michael didn't have to, either, but she didn't want to argue with him over this. Sometimes it was nice to just have someone want to. It was getting late but she was having such a good time she really didn't want the night to end.

They settled the check and Michael tried to feel out the situation. Should he walk her home? Where was home? Should he call it a night and ask her to dinner?

"So, I know it's late, but I really am not quite ready for the night to end," he said.

Beth looked at him and reached behind the bar and grabbed the opened bottle of wine and two wine glasses.

Michael raised an eyebrow.

Beth had a slightly devilish grin on her lips. "Follow me," she said. Wow, she thought to herself as Michael followed her out the back door of the Tavern. She had some serious liquid confidence tonight. The summer air was still warm and felt nice on her skin, but she was comfortable in her oxford shirt and jeans. They walked through the plush grass to a private corner of the Inn's yard. There were two Adirondack chairs there. Perfect for stargazing, and other activities best left to the moonlight, thought Beth.

They had walked in silence, and in silence Beth gestured for Michael to sit. She poured them each a glass of wine and then settled into her chair. Michael sipped his glass of wine and stared at her intently.

Michael took another sip of his wine and then placed it aside. He decided she was too far away; he needed to close the gap between them. He pulled his chair around so that he was directly in front of her and their knees were touching. He was on the edge of his seat, wondering what he should do next.

"I'm nervous," she blurted.

Beth's statement caught Michael off guard, but it also made him smile. "You don't say." His tone was low and amused and he was watching her intently. "And why is that?"

"Because I'm trying to figure out if this is a good idea or not, and you're looking at me," she said as she watched him with a mixture of anticipation, desire and heat that was unfamiliar. She wanted him. Michael's movement interrupted her thoughts. He had leaned forward and he was looking at her intensely.

The silence between them had turned so absolute that all Michael could hear was the wind whistling behind him and if he listened carefully, he could hear Beth's heart beating almost as fast as his own. She leaned closer and reached across and grabbed his hands in hers.

All the blood in his body rushed straight to his groin. Despite all the years it had been, one thing had not changed. All Beth had to do was look at him and his body would respond.

Their eyes connected in the semi-darkness and held. He leaned in and their lips met, molding together, tongues tangling, the heat building between them. They stayed like that for many moments until Beth rose and sat in Michael's lap, feeling his hardness. She smiled and kissed him.

Michael responded with a groan and his arms encircled her and his hands roamed over her body, encountering what he thought was far too many layers of material.

"These need to come off," Michael said breaking the silence and he began to unbutton her oxford shirt all while kissing her neck and then her lips.

Beth let out a soft moan. It had been a long time since she had been kissed like this and who would have ever thought she'd be kissing Michael! He certainly had changed since high school, she thought, as her hands roamed his body. His back was like one large muscle, his shoulders broad, despite his lean frame. His chest muscles and stomach muscles were tight. His arms were strong and she liked how they felt circling around her. She was feeling warm inside and had a desire deep inside to do more than just kiss. This was getting intense. Beth wasn't sure she was ready for this — it had been such a long time since she had been with someone and that fact made her nervous.

Beth removed her arms from where they were resting around Michael's neck and placed them on his chest. Then she pushed him away lightly, and then more forcefully, bringing their kiss to an end.

Michael looked into to her eyes,

She sighed. "I should get you home."

Michael looked crestfallen. She didn't want to hurt him but this was just moving too fast. On top of that, tomorrow was the first night of the bike tour at the Inn and it was her chance to impress them and get a contract booking that could lead to some press and reviews that could help her grow the Inn. It was all too much to risk for a man who was likely leaving in two weeks.

"Is everything okay, Beth? Did I do something wrong? I hope you don't think I was trying to push for anything we're both not ready for." He looked at her, searching her eyes, to see what she was thinking, what she was feeling.

"No, you didn't do anything wrong, and I didn't think that. It's just that—" how was she going to word this? Michael was great, he was good-looking, smart, successful, nice, sexy, sincere … basically everything she would normally want in a man. But there were no guarantee he would be here in two weeks. Not that she needed a guarantee. But she couldn't risk a great business opportunity for a fling. And frankly, she was tired of being left. First her parents, then her sister, and then strings of boyfriends.

"It's just that I have a big day at the Inn tomorrow and a special tasting menu to prepare and …"

Michael interrupted her before she could finish, "Say no more. You have an important day tomorrow and I don't want to get in the way. But maybe we can go out one night, or one afternoon? Whatever works best with your schedule here at the Inn?"

She looked hesitant, but something in her eyes gave Michael hope that tonight wasn't a lark.

"You don't have to tell me now. Let it marinate, okay? I'd really like to see you again."

It was hard to say no to that sexy smile. She felt her whole body grow warm. She leaned in and gave him a quick kiss on the lips and smiled at him before standing up.

Michael was confused but he also understood. He was always so focused on his career and would never let a woman get in the way of his work — it seemed like Beth was the same way. It's funny how sometimes the very thing that draws you to someone is the thing that could keep you away from them. But he wasn't going to give up, they had something and maybe it was only physical but maybe that was all either of them could handle now, anyway.

CHAPTER NINE

Argghh ... the world was ending. At least that's how Michael felt. He had way too much to drink the night before. Drinking that much was never worth it the next day, he thought. However, it was all worth it for the moments he and Beth had shared behind the Inn. He wasn't sure if she would want to see him again but he knew what he wanted and he intended to go after it. Beth was intriguing — she was smart, funny, driven, and attractive — something he had yet to find within one woman. But he needed to put her out of his mind for the day, since it was going to be a busy one.

The shingle guys would be arriving that morning and Jonah would be supervising them. Michael would probably have to tell his mother about what he and Annie had discovered about Malone's Market. He wasn't planning on visiting his Dad that day but it was certainly weighing on him. And to top it off, he was babysitting. Some vacation. He looked over at the alarm clock and jumped up. It was already six forty-five! Annie would be here any minute. He shot out of bed and in a matter of five minutes, he had showered and pulled on jeans with a navy blue t-shirt, a brown belt, sunglasses, and his brown boat shoes. He quickly looked at himself in the mirror. He had stubble but he knew he'd have no time to shave with Annie on the way. He grabbed his wallet and keys and by the time he hit the bottom of the stairs, Annie was knocking on the door.

He opened it and before he could say a word, Annie said, "God, you look like hell!"

Michael growled at her and simply said, "Need coffee," as he pulled on his sunglasses.

"Ah-Ah, little brother, details, details!"

They both walked to the car and Michael got in on the passenger side. He buckled in before saying, "Not much to tell. We were having a great time chatting, we even kissed—"

"Whoa! Not much to tell. Sounds like a lot to me," Annie said, as she started the car and pulled out of the driveway to head to the market.

"Yeah, I know. She just, you know, hit the breaks fast and basically said she's busy with work. I don't know, we'll see. I'll give her a little space. Anyway, now how about that coffee?"

They pulled into the Dunkin Donuts and each got a coffee. Michael also opted for a chocolate glazed donut, something his trainer would have killed him for. He also hadn't worked out once since he got there almost six days ago. That needed to change. He'd plan to finally put on those running shoes he'd brought with him and workout. He sipped his coffee as Annie drove and by the time they got to Malone's Market, he felt almost human again. She promised him that they would be continuing the conversation about his night later that afternoon before his babysitting duty began.

He and Annie agreed that he'd be spending all day in the office. He'd try to get a filing system going and pay the most important bills he could. In the afternoon, they'd speak to their mother. Michael also needed to think about when he was going to face his Dad again. It had only been two days but it felt like an eternity.

When Michael walked in, he waved to the cashiers, including his sister Judy, and then he headed up the stairs, still sipping his coffee. When he got to his father's office, he saw someone else was already there and the computer was on. It was his mother and it looked like she was crying. She turned around as she heard Michael approach.

"So, I was right, but I had no idea how right I was." She had opened up his spreadsheet with the profit and loss calculations. "Michael, what are we going to do? I think this just might be what caused your father's stroke. I can't believe he didn't share any of this with me. I could have helped. I don't know how, but maybe I could have convinced him to slow down on the improvements — oh, it's just such a mess."

She began to sob.

Michael crossed the room and set down his coffee. Today of all days and first thing in the morning, too. He put his arms around his mother and held her while she cried. They stood there for a while until Marty broke the connection and wiped her eyes with her sleeve.

"It's all making sense now, Michael. I am so angry with him. Why couldn't he share this with us, why couldn't he ask for help? He is just so goddamned stubborn."

Michael was beginning to think his father knew exactly what had happened, but he couldn't say that. Instead, he said, "Mom, sometimes when you encounter stuff like this and you're in it, you can't see just how bad it really is. I know we can save Malone's Market, though, if Dad will let me help. I actually think if we all helped and put our ideas together as a family, we can really make things work."

Marty sighed but then a look of determination crossed her face. "Write up your ideas, son. We're going to talk to your father about this and let's see how many months we can make it until we come up with a formal plan."

"Mom, I can help a little. I can pay—"

"Michael, no. Don't think I didn't realize what you've already paid for at the house. Although I appreciate that, this is too much to ask and even too much money for you to put up. Unless ..." she paused and had a thoughtful look on her face. "Unless you become a partner in the business ... and that's not something I think you've ever had an interest in. And that would be something everyone, including your Dad, would need to think about ... but that could really work ... just think of it as an investment."

Become a partner! That was not something that had even crossed Michael's mind. He guessed he was enjoying himself this week but being here permanently would be difficult, especially once his Dad was back. Michael suddenly felt scared, what if his father didn't come back? He really did need to go speak with him, and he needed to do it alone.

"Mom, I'm not really sure how I would feel about all of that, but I do know I want to help and that I do care about the fate of the business. Let me take a look at all of the finances and come up with a plan. It might take me a few days but I think I have some ideas and I would love to sit with all of you: you, Annie, Jonah, and Judy, and see what all your thoughts are. I think everyone could really have good ideas and talents we haven't tapped into. For instance, why haven't we made a website when we have Jonah here? Why aren't we serving your delicious lobster rolls to the public — if you ask me, depriving the public of those is a crime."

Marty smiled for the first time that morning and punched Michael on the shoulder. "Flattery will get you everywhere!"

He smiled at his mother and said, "Okay, well I guess I better get to it, especially since I'm ducking out early today to get some supplies for babysitting the boys."

His mother left him alone in the office and Michael sat down and stared at the spreadsheet. He decided to get any additional data into Excel and then begin filing and color-coding. He loved these types of tasks. Of course he loved to be challenged, too, but sometimes it was nice to get visible results right away. Maybe that's why Beth liked cooking so much, he thought. Originally, when they were in high school, she had talked quite a bit about becoming a doctor. He had to admit that she had been a great lab partner and probably would have made a great doctor, but he was actually more impressed that she became a chef.

Once upon a time he thought he'd be a writer. Instead, he picked his career by picking what he was best at and what he would make the most money doing. At the end of the day, finance and the market didn't make him happy. He was good at it, he had good instincts and he was comfortable taking financial risks — but for some reason, not creative ones. He really admired Beth for taking the unexpected route and coming back and creating something great for the town. Not only did her Inn provide jobs, it also was a place where the townspeople could convene.

As he was getting his family's things in order, he also decided it was time for him to take charge of his life, too, and really think about his next steps. He picked up the phone again and tried his assistant. He checked his email, nothing. He knew it was over. He just had to decide what he was going to do about it, and come to terms with it all and with what he wanted to do next. But honestly, for some reason he didn't care that much about his job and what could happen, maybe that should tell him something. The money may be great, better than great, but he felt empty at the end of the day. Something to think about.

When he looked at the clock, it was nearly noon. Michael looked around the office and noted that he had placed the last files into the file cabinets. They were labeled and color-coded. That just left the stack of bills, which he was going to take care of next. He sat down and took a look at each of them carefully before he wrote out any checks. He set aside some of the smaller, less noticeable bills to pay for the next day, with his own checkbook. Just a little help to keep the place going. He wished he could just give his family the $500,000 — but his had mother had made it clear that she felt if he did, then he should have a stake in the business.

Even though he had made and saved millions of dollars, a half million was not exactly a small expense. He had all of the important and urgent bills paid and some set aside for the next day, when both Annie and his mother came in armed with tuna salad sandwiches, colas, and chips.

"So, Mom and I talked," Annie said. "We have a number of ideas for improvements that might not be so costly, based on what we've heard on the floor from customers."

Michael listened carefully as his mother and sister offered some suggestions. A deli counter, recipe cards at the fish counter suggesting their other products, more appropriate seafood accompaniments, pre-packaged foods, a small coffee shop with its own separate register and entrance.

Michael also shared a few of his own ideas, a re-branding effort, new logo, picnic tables out back, and an ocean-themed playground area for kids. He wanted to make the Market a destination and help set it apart from the competition.

They were all good ideas, and many of them wouldn't be nearly as expensive as some of the things their father had put in place, including large tanks for fish that spanned floor to ceiling ... making Malone's more like sea world than a market. There were clearly some misguided plans that were going to take place — but they could change that.

Marty took a deep breath. "I think we have some good ideas here but we're going to have to talk to your father about all of this, and you know how stubborn he is. And he's never listened to any of us..."

Michael knew what was coming.

Annie looked at their mother. "You should really talk to him, Mikey. I know things are rough between you two, but believe it or not, I think Dad will listen to you. You wouldn't be so successful managing that hedge fund if you didn't have a head for business. We need that."

His mother gave him a meaningful look. He didn't know what to say. He was honored that they valued him but he also wasn't sure he wanted to work at Malone's, and he definitely didn't want to speak to his father about all of this. But he saw no way around it.

"Fine, I'll talk to him. And I am happy to help, but I don't know that I want to be a part of Malone's Market full-time, but we can work something out."

Both his mother and Annie smiled.

Michael said, "So, I'm going to wrap things up, Annie, and then I'm going to go get some pizzas and videos and head over to your place to see the boys."

"Sounds good. Tom will be there, he'll give you the rundown on bedtimes, baths, and all that. Thanks again, Michael. We're looking forward to some alone time." She winked and Michael nearly gagged. As much as he liked his sister, even at thirty-one, sometimes he just did not need the details about her personal life, even just implied details.

***

Beth was tired. Making breakfast that morning was hell on earth. Her head was pounding and she felt like she had cotton in her mouth from being so dehydrated. And she kept getting distracted while baking; she nearly burned her scones. All she could do was think of Michael. Why couldn't she get him out of her head? Sure, he had lean muscles and long limbs, sure he had deep blue eyes and dark hair and a smile that could make you weak in the knees — but she wasn't interested. She couldn't be. She had no time for this, and she certainly had no time for someone who was just going to up and leave in a few weeks. Where would that leave her? She couldn't think about it anymore, she had too much work to do. And she told herself that she wasn't interested, not interested at all. So why did she keep seeing his face everywhere and keep replaying last night over and over in her head? She sighed.

Okay, fine, she liked him. She was really interested, but he was leaving soon. She knew he said he thought about leaving his job and coming back ... but thinking about doing something and actually doing something were two entirely different things. But if she just thought of it as a fling, maybe it would be better. It had been quite some time since she had been with someone and she didn't know how much longer she could take it. She was independent, but being alone was not always the most fulfilling. She sighed again.

"Oh, mother — damn it." She had just burned the asparagus for her vegetable frittata. Today's breakfast special. She needed to focus; she needed to get him out of her head. She couldn't keep thinking about Michael with all the pending guests. As much as she loved the restaurant and the Tavern, it was the Inn that brought in the greatest profit margins. Impressing a tour group like Pedal Feet was exactly what she needed to allow the Warren to thrive. Today bicycle tours, tomorrow weddings, she thought. And as far as Michael — well, if he really did ever move to Maine, then maybe they could have something. But until then, if it ever happened, she needed to focus.

She needed to get through this breakfast first and then she'd be off to town to get the items necessary to welcome her guest. She was thinking little bags with bottles of water, power bars, other Maine snacks, and a copy of DownEast Magazine would be a nice welcome for her guests. She loved the idea, but too bad she had only thought of it this morning, and right before breakfast service was about to begin.

After breakfast service, she met with the staff, then Lisa arrived and all plans were in place for the welcome reception for their guests in the Tavern that evening. They'd be serving a simple fare for their first evening in Gray Harbor, the Tavern's standard menu. The only difference was they'd have some passed hors d'oeuvres during the welcome cocktail hour from five thirty to seven thirty that evening. When all was set, it was already two... Beth had to hurry before the check-ins in two hours; they decided to hand out the bags at check-in, so she needed to do some fast shopping first. She grabbed her purse and keys from her office behind the kitchen and made her way to her car.

***

After lunch, Michael wrapped up some paperwork and saved it all on the computer. He also printed out suggestion slips and made a customer feedback box for the front of the store. He thought that he, his mother, and Annie had come up with a lot of good ideas, but he wanted to hear from their customer base, maybe they saw flaws in the business that his family did not. Maybe there were more products they'd like Malone's to carry, maybe they thought the checkout lines were not efficient enough. As he made his way to the parking lot, he called Jonah to check in.

"Jonah, how's it going?"

"Mikey! Hey! Man, it's looking good. These shingles are nice. Oh, and your friend Bob from the store is here. He threw in some window boxes with flowers that he's installing. They have geraniums or something in them. Whatever it is, Mom will love it. It's like a whole crew is here. They're doing the front and sides of the house today and he says they'll wrap up tomorrow."

"That's great, Jonah, just great. Hey, I wanted to talk to you about something" said Michael in a deliberate way.

"Yeah, what's up?" responded Jonah cautiously.

Michael decided to get right to the point. "Have you ever made a website? I think we should have one for Malone's and I was hoping you could help. "

"I mean, I could, but that would take a lot of time..."

"What if I cover some of your hours at the fish market in exchange and you still get paid? You'll just work upstairs in the office instead."

There was a pause as Jonah considered it. Then he said, "All right, cool, but we should also maybe do a Facebook page, a Twitter feed, and maybe even a Pinterest page about new products or from the perspective of a fishmonger. Oh, wait, we could even do our coupons from it and save money instead of that old circular—"

Michael was impressed. "Wow, Jonah, this all sounds great. Have you ever talked to Dad about these ideas?"

Jonah chuckled. "Are you kidding me! Like he would ever listen."

"Well, let's do it. Why don't we sit together tomorrow afternoon and talk. I'd like to hear your ideas on re-branding, too, and let's get Judy involved in that. What do you think?"

"That sounds awesome! I'll ask Judy what she can do with the logo. She is great with all that graphic design stuff."

"She is?"

"Oh, yeah, loves it, she wants to go to art school. Oh, crap, I wasn't supposed to say anything. Anyway, I'll talk to her about it today! Talk to you later, bro!" With that, Jonah hung up.

Huh, Michael thought, as he started the car. Looks like he wasn't the only one who thought their father was stubborn. And even Judy was afraid to tell the family what she'd really like to do. He began to think maybe a mural might be nice touch on the wall in the parking lot near where he and his mother ate lunch the other day. Judy could probably help with that, too. That wall was just large concrete bricks. Rather than painting it or siding it, a mural could give the place a nice whimsical feel, especially along with a small jungle gym … or maybe just some swings, since they would mean less liability. Maybe he would talk to his mother and Judy about that. He had so many thoughts swimming around his head that he didn't realize he had arrived at the video store, which was next to an old bookstore. He decided to stop in to the bookstore first, but stopped when he noticed a large 'for sale' sign outside of the building.

"I can't believe it," he mumbled. He had spent many years in the bookstore when he was young and even all these years later, the place still looked magical. It was a small stone structure that had three levels.

Mrs. Slossenger, the owner, had moved into the basement when her husband had passed away and the other two floors housed books. He peered through the windows and saw the shelves and the tables. He had spent so much time there growing up, but he guessed with the advent of the e-reader and the Internet, books were less popular. But with all the tourists, he figured mass-market paperbacks and magazines would still sell. He didn't know why he did it but he opened up his wallet and took out a card so he could jot down the number on the 'for sale' sign. It couldn't hurt to find out how much the place was ... even as a vacation apartment. He could remodel and take the top floor as an apartment and rent out the other two floors to a store. It could be a nice investment. It would be small, but surely bigger than his studio in New York. He whistled as he walked over to the video store.

After thirty minutes, he walked out with what he thought would be a good assortment of movies and snacks for his nephews, who were five, seven, and eight years old. He got two Harry Potter movies, the latest Pirates of the Caribbean, Narnia, and a super hero movie. He looked at his watch. It was three forty-five. A little too early to buy the pizza now, so he grabbed a menu and made sure they did delivery. Next stop, the drug store. He figured comic books and soda would be good. He also wanted a new notebook and some more pens for himself. He was making his way down the aisles with his arms full of 'supplies,' when a woman bumped right into him. He was annoyed.

"Hey, watch where you're going," he said, before he realized the woman was Beth. She looked startled.

"Sorry about that, I'm in the biggest rush," she said, without even looking up.

"Beth? Hey, it's me, Michael, no problem. You okay? Anything I can help you with?"

Oh, God, she thought, it's him. The last person she wanted to see when she was so frantic. She was trying to find enough copies of DownEast Magazine for her gift bags and couldn't. She was freaking out.

"Well, I need twelve copies of DownEast Magazine but there are only four here, and there really isn't anywhere else in town to pick it up ... I need them for these gift bags for the guests. But there aren't any ... and now I don't know what to do." Her words came out in a rush.

"You know what, I saw some by the register. I'll be right back and see if they have eight more." With that, Michael ran off to the register and saw some right by checkout. He grabbed them and he also grabbed a bag of individually wrapped Maine candies. He left his own items for purchase at the counter and let them know he'd be right back. He ran back to Beth with his finds. She was still franticly looking on the ground. He bent down beside her and handed her the magazines.

"Here, I found eight more, and I thought if you're making bags for guests that maybe these little maple candies might be nice, too." He placed them in her basket and looked at her.

Beth was relieved, she hadn't even thought of

checking the checkout counter. She never bothered because all she ever noticed were the copies of People Magazine and US Weekly. She was glad Michael found them but also annoyed. She was hoping to avoid him entirely. She got up and so did he.

"Well thanks, Michael, I appreciate it," she said cordially.

Michael looked taken aback. Despite how the previous night had ended, he thought they shared something. And although he was nervous, he wasn't going to give up.

"So, um, Beth, I was wondering. I know you're pretty busy this weekend, but would you like to have dinner some time, or lunch? Maybe Sunday night?"

"Michael, I like you but I just don't know if it's a good idea. You're leaving Gray Harbor soon and I'm not really looking for a fling..." She let her voice trail off.

So that was what she was worried about, he thought. "How about dinner as friends, then? I really enjoyed chatting with you last night. At the very least, I'd like to continue to catch up, maybe even get some advice from you on what it's like being a business person in Gray Harbor. Let's just call it a business lunch instead, then, how about that? Can I pick you up at one o'clock Sunday?"

She looked like she was thinking it over, but he could tell she wanted to say yes. "Okay, fine, but only because it's a business lunch and we're meeting as friends."

His confidence restored, he smiled and said, "Of course, I'm looking forward to it. Good luck with your guests, I'll see you Sunday!" He waved as she walked away towards the checkout.

He quickly looked at his watch and saw that it was almost time to go babysit. He ran to the checkout and made his purchases, then headed for the car. He had promised to be at his sister's house by five and he didn't want to let Annie or Tom down. They needed the night alone and he needed the chance to get better acquainted with his nephews.

CHAPTER TEN

Michael was in awe of his sister. How did she do it every day? He had spent five hours with her three sons and was wiped out. After he arrived at Annie and Tom's home, Tom showed Michael the ropes, pointing out where everything was from snacks to toothbrushes and pajamas.

Tom was a cool guy, thought Michael. He was quiet and reserved but you could just tell he had a sense of humor. Tom was on leave due to an injury. He had broken his arm in a 'silly accident' while training his plebes down at a boot camp in Portland. Tom said he was thinking of taking it easy and maybe becoming a recruiter so he could finish out his remaining two years with the Navy before retiring and then moving on to something else. But as Tom said, right now he was focused on being a father and a husband, and as fun as the Navy was, he said nothing could be more fun than hanging out with his three sons.

Fun? Michael thought that the night of babysitting certainly wasn't fun. Okay, well, that wasn't entirely true; he did have fun with the kids, but he also realized that three boys was a lot of work.

He got reacquainted with his nephews when he

got there and each of them gave him a tour of his room. Then they ordered pizza and played video games and drank sodas until the pizzas arrived. Michael learned the error in his ways after dinner, when they were all hyped up from so much caffeine. He gave piggy back rides, helped make model planes, watched pieces of each of the movies he brought till they got bored, and basically ran around like a madman. At around nine thirty they all started losing steam, so Michael put them to bed. Finally it was quiet. He could hear himself think.

He was tired but he also could see why people wanted to have families. It felt really rewarding. And amid all the commotion tonight, he felt like he imparted some important lessons on the boys. Why black magic was always bad and why you should always have a napkin on your lap while eating pizza (in case the hot cheese fell off). He thought maybe someday he could get into this whole father and husband thing like Tom. What a scary thought!

And speaking of fathers, Michael thought about his own as he cleaned up the mess in the kitchen. He needed to clear the air with his father. He decided he was going to do it tomorrow morning before he wimped out. It had gone on for too long. He had a feeling that maybe his father wouldn't feel the need to be such a tough guy if they were alone. Maybe they could talk it out. And maybe they could even discuss how they could save Malone's.

Michael also began thinking about his work. No one had called him back. He had left messages, sent emails. It felt like he was getting the silent treatment. He made a mental calculation of what was in his savings accounts outside of his investments — six million dollars, give or take a few thousand. He could comfortably resign and forget about all of the headaches he'd been dealing with at the fund. They all referred to themselves as the Goldfarb Family — but they weren't family; hell, they weren't even his friends. Not a soul had gotten back to him. He was going to have to go back to New York and resign in person. It was over and it was okay. He wasn't sure what was next, but he did know that he needed a change.

He just wasn't satisfied with his career anymore. But he did like being a part of something important. He also liked being a part of the family again. It was something he hadn't felt like in a long time ... not since Jesse had died. It hadn't been the same -- or maybe it had just been Michael who wasn't the same. He sat on the sofa and did something he hadn't done in a long time, read the paper.

***

Beth breathed a sigh of relief. Night one was over and it had been a hit. Everyone loved the bags, the hors d'oeuvres, and the cocktail hour. The dining room had a number of guests in it and as usual, the Tavern was doing quite well for a Thursday evening. The head of the touring group had said to her if the rest of the week went as well as tonight did, then they'd like to reserve group holidays on a consistent basis with as many as twenty-four guests in a single weekend! It would be a dream come true for Beth. That would account for a nice little chunk of annual expenses. She was going to sleep well tonight, and tomorrow she would go for a nice jog and maybe even go sit out by the lighthouse after breakfast was served.

The tour guide really thought the bags were a nice touch, especially the candies. He even offered to pay a little extra for some additional items to be added to the bags, including brochures, bike maps, and anything else that could also be "very Maine." Maybe she would get some of Michael's ideas during their 'business lunch' on Sunday. She wondered what she should wear and where they would be going. Knowing the only other restaurants in town were informal, she decided casual would be the right look. What was she thinking? Why was she even thinking about this? She was not interested in Michael. Now that her mind was convinced, she just needed to convince her body of that, because every time she thought of him she felt an undeniable heat in her abdomen and her heart beat faster. She guessed there was nothing wrong with admiring him. He was like a taller, more muscular Patrick Dempsey ... and who could say no to that? She meant, who couldn't look at that? No, she thought, she couldn't do this. She had more important things to do than get involved with a man who wouldn't be sticking around.

***

The next morning, Michael got up early and got dressed to go running. Visiting hours at the hospital began at noon that day and he planned to be there then but before that, he had some other things to attend to at home. He had hired some painters to finish the work he and Jonah had started on the inside. He had also asked Bob to stop by with some slipcovers for the old sofas and see what he could come up with in terms of sprucing up the decor. He placed Judy in charge of taking care of that today. He was going to check out the work being done on the exterior of the house and he had also hired someone from McAllister's to do some planting and gardening. The place was really starting to come together.

He ran downstairs and had a little coffee, let in the painters, and set up the rest of the workers around the house. Before he knew it, it was nine o'clock. He decided to head off in the direction of the Warren Inn and the Gray Harbor Lighthouse.

He was feeling out of shape by the time he had run the three miles to the lighthouse. A few weeks ago, he wouldn't have even been winded, he realized. He decided to have a little break, have a drink, and sit by the water. Just behind the lighthouse, there were these beautiful boulders right by the ocean where tourists often sat and watched the boats go by. In the distance, you could frequently see lobster boats. At this time of day, many of the lobsterman would have already been out for several hours but you could probably still see a few from the lighthouse.

Michael walked by the small lighthouse and thought about how when he was a child, he had imagined living in a lighthouse of his very own someday. He had also dreamed of being a lobsterman, a naval officer, and a bag boy at Malone's Market. Funny how hedge fund manager had never occurred to him. He smiled at himself.

He walked out to the boulders and was climbing down when he saw her. There was Beth, sitting on the very edge of a sloping stone, with her feet partially in the water and partially on the pebbled beach surrounding the lighthouse. You could only ever see the little beach when it was low tide.

"Pardon me, is this seat taken?" he asked her.

She looked startled but before she could stop herself, she smiled and said flirtatiously, "So ... are you stalking me? First the market, then the tavern, the drugstore, and now here at the lighthouse? Come on, Malone, be a little more subtle."

He had to laugh at that one. She looked at him, amused.

"Beth, I'm shocked that you would even imply that. I think you must have Annie feeding you the details of my whereabouts. I always run in the mornings, and who wouldn't run to the lighthouse? It's gorgeous here."

"Okay, okay. I'll let it slide this time," she said with a smile, as she shaded her eyes from the sun.

She looked great. She had on short navy blue running shorts with orange stripes. She wore a tight, white tank top, white cross-trainers, and her hair was up in a ponytail. She looked healthy and even fairly tan for a redhead.

He took a breath and looked out at the water. They sat in silence for a few moments. Then he asked, "So, how did it go last night?"

She looked surprised that he remembered or even cared. Usually the men she went out with weren't very interested in the happenings at the Inn. But then again, since they were 'friends' she supposed that was a normal question. Surely Annie would ask her such a thing. Now she was even rambling in her thoughts.

"It went really well, thanks again for your help."

"I didn't do anything really," he paused as she was

about to protest, "but I'm glad it went well." He glanced at her shyly.

She filled him in on what the tour guide had said and Michael shared in her enthusiasm. He even offered up a great idea.

"You should get some bikes for the Inn, you could rent them out or let guests use them for free so they can ride up to the lighthouse or even go into town instead of driving. I think people could get into that, and it would show how bike friendly you are. And you could get some fairly inexpensive cruiser bikes online."

"That's a great idea," said Beth. And she really meant it. She hadn't heard of any other Inn doing such a thing, so it could really help her get a write up by DownEast or even other travel magazines. It always helped to have a distinguishing characteristic. Maybe a business lunch with Michael on Sunday wouldn't be such a bad idea after all. She really enjoyed speaking with him. They stayed there for a while just chatting until he looked at his watch.

"Time really flies when I'm with you," he said. "It's already eleven thirty. I need to head back and go visit my father at the hospital."

He looked serious for a moment and then his face brightened. "This has been really nice. I'm really looking forward to Sunday. Dress casual. We aren't going anywhere fancy for our lunch but I think you'll like it."

He offered her his hand so she could get up, too. She took it and they both climbed the boulders together. When they reached the top, Beth stumbled and Michael caught her, and then he did a very unprofessional thing. He looked in her eyes and kissed her on the lips.

His lips were soft and his arms strong around her. She forgot her surroundings.

"Goodbye, see you Sunday!" And with that he ran off.

Beth just stood there dumfounded as he ran off. What just happened? Did he really just kiss her? She began jogging back to the Warren Inn with a stupid smile on her face. Even though she was feeling really cautious about this whole thing, maybe she shouldn't. Maybe she should just live in the moment and enjoy Michael while he was here. It wasn't often she met a man with whom she shared such mutual attraction, intense chemistry, and great conversations. Maybe she should just go for it?

Although she had no problem taking risks with her cuisine, with her business, or even at times with her own personal fashion, she had always guarded herself when it came to men. Maybe it was her parents' terrible relationship. She remembered the day her parents had died in a car accident. They had been arguing even before they got in the car to take her older sister on a college visit.

It had been raining and they crashed into a truck. Her sister made it out alive somehow but her parents had died instantly. She remembered that awful day now as she slowed to a walk. She had been called out of class to the principal's office. Then months later, she got that call again after sister's accident. Her sister had been on life support for several days before she finally let go. When she got the call that her sister was gone for good, Michael had slipped out of class to see if she was all right. She sobbed and told him everything.

Things she had never told her friends about her parents, about finding out her father had had an affair. About how she had told her mother the night before. About how their death was probably her fault, and about how now Jen, who had nearly lost her life months before, had died in another tragic accident and how she couldn't stop it. She begged him not to tell anyone, and he never did. He never even mentioned it again. She had mostly blocked that out. But as she walked beyond the Inn and into her cottage, she realized that maybe knowing what she knew about her parents' marriage was why she was so distrustful of men. Maybe it was why she would never let anyone close.

But she had that one time. That one time in high school, she had let in nerdy, pepperoni-faced Malone. Maybe it was time now to let in Michael, the man. She smiled slightly at the thought and then hit the shower.

***

Michael ran all the way home at full speed. He was glad he had run into Beth and that they had shared a moment, but now he had to stay focused. He needed to figure out what he was going to say to his father and how he would patch things up, if they could be patched up at all. He was also concerned about broaching the topic of the business. By the time he arrived back at the house, he was breathless. He quickly waved to Jonah, who was working in the kitchen on his laptop. Jonah looked like he wanted to talk but Michael avoided it. He saw Judy and Bob, who were in a deep conversation about color palettes and said a quick hello as he ran to the shower. He showered quickly and opted against shaving. He had always wanted to grow a beard; maybe he'd just go with it. He threw on some jeans, a fresh green polo shirt, his boat shoes, and Wayfarer sunglasses. In ten minutes flat he was clean and dressed and in his car.

On the ride over to the hospital, Michael couldn't help but replay the interaction he had with his dad on Monday over and over again in his head. When his dad had said he didn't want to see Michael. Would today be any different? Michael took in a deep breath as he pulled into the Saint Andrews parking lot. He had no idea how this was going to go but he knew it had to happen. He walked to the front desk and found out his father's room number, then made his way up the elevator. Once he got to his father's door, he stood outside it for a few minutes, trying to compose himself, when his father's doctor walked out of the room.

"Can I help you?" She asked, holding her clipboard.

Michael looked at her name tag before responding, "Yes, Dr. Williams, I was just going in to say hi to my father."

"Oh, yes." She smiled. "You must be Michael, the big finance guy in New York. Your dad will be happy to see you, just go right in."

Huh? His father talked about him to his doctor? Michael couldn't believe it, especially after Monday. He took a deep breath and walked in slowly. He saw his father lying there a bit dazed, just watching television.

"Hello, Dad," said Michael hesitantly.

His father said nothing but looked at Michael and a light seemed to flicker in his eyes before darkening again. But he said nothing. There was a chair by his bed and Michael went over and sat down.

"Dad, I know you didn't want to see me Monday and I don't know if you want to see me today. But I wanted to see you." He paused and looked at his father. His father had turned his head slightly to see Michael better and was focusing on what he was saying. He didn't say anything but Michael could tell that he could hear him. Michael let out a sigh.

"Dad, thirteen years ago I left because I wanted to live my dream. I wanted to go to New York and make something out of myself, like you did for yourself in Maine. I've worked really hard at what I've been doing but I think I want to do something else now."

He took a deep breath before continuing. "Being back home this week has inspired me and I want to try a new endeavor. But first …" Michael took another breath and looked at his father. His father had a hopeful, but also extremely sad, look in his blue eyes. He almost looked vulnerable, something Michael never thought he'd be able to say about his father.

Michael repeated himself again. "But first," he paused and said, "I want to help out with Malone's Market and make the whole family's dream come true and finish putting Malone's on the map. And I also wanted to say..." he faltered a bit and paused.

"I'm sorry, Dad. I'm sorry for all the time we've lost together as father and son because I've been too stubborn about all of this."

Michael looked at his father, who was struggling to move his lips. Finally, his dad said in a strained tone, "It's okay, son." It took a lot out of him to say the words. He paused and said, "I na na need you annnnda ammm gladda you are here." A tear streamed down

James Malone's face. Something Michael had never seen before. His father — the strongest and toughest man in the world — was crying. Michael couldn't believe it. He got up from his seat and went over and hugged his Dad, starting to cry, too. He knew what he had to do now. He had to fix this. After a few moments, he sat back down and looked at his Dad and held his hand. It was limp, but Michael sat there and held it and listened to his father.

"Sonna I am sorry tatatoo. I na na needa your help. The markmarkettta is in trubtruble." James fought to get the words out.

"Dad, I know. I've been helping out this past week and know all about it. But there is a solution, Dad. If you trust me to work on it with you and the rest of the family."

James attempted a smile again. "Soundsa good, whattaver yooou thinthink. I am afraida...gotta ina over my head."

"Dad, I have a lot of ideas but I don't want to do anything without your consent. How about I work out some ideas and I come here each day and we can go over the plans and make some decisions together? As partners, if you like."

James smiled again and slowly formulated his next words. "That's ppperrrfeccct, son."

Michael smiled and embraced his dad one more time before heading out. James Malone looked happy and Michael felt happier than he had in a long time. In fact, he felt like a million pound weight had been lifted off his back. He looked at his watch and saw that it was already three thirty. This entire day had flown by.

Before heading out, Michael went to find Dr.

Williams to discuss his father's treatment and find out what would be necessary at home and how he would be able to navigate through life with this now.

Dr. Williams explained that James had already started rehabilitation at the health center, which was expensive but worth it. She told him that his father had started to walk, which was huge, but that the next three to four weeks were going to be key and he would need all the support he could get. That meant daily visits and support, maybe even some help during physical therapy. Speech and balance might take longer and he might never be able to use his left hand fully but Dr. Williams said she thought James was very lucky. If it hadn't been for Marty's early discovery of James it would have been much worse. Some more changes would need to be made to help James transition back home and back to the store. Michael knew he could help make it work.

Michael walked to the car and called his mother at the market and told her he had visited his father. She was ecstatic. He told her he would pick up some pizzas and other goodies and get things ready for dinner at seven that night. Next he called Jonah to ask what videos or games he might want and to let him know they could discuss the website when Michael got home. Then Michael drove into town feeling better than he had in a long time.

CHAPTER ELEVEN

After leaving the hospital, Michael ran a few errands in town including grabbing some soda, videos and video games, pizzas, pasta, and salads. He also grabbed the Wall Street Journal for the hell of it; maybe he'd dig into it later tonight or the next day and see what was happening with the markets.

When he drove home he liked what he saw. The siding had been finished, window boxes with beautiful flowers had been put in, and the lawn looked well manicured. Flowers were planted everywhere. It looked kind of like it had when they were kids, but better. Michael went in and unloaded everything on the table and then looked for Judy and Jonah. He walked into the living room to find Judy sitting in there with her sketchpad.

"Hey, Judy, how's it going?"

"Hey, Mikey. I'm just sketching a few things. Jonah told me you wanted a new logo and maybe even some rebranding for the market, so I'm kicking around a few ideas."

"Cool! Hey, you know what, I think this is the first time I've ever seen anyone sit in this room."

"Oh yeah, they're repainting the den. Did you

know it used to be a master bedroom? That's what Bob told me. He's doing it in a grayish-cream color so that we can really have some fun decorating in there, or even turn it into a bedroom when Dad gets home from the hospital. So anyway, I've been sitting in here while they're working."

"Huh, that's a great idea about the bedroom. So, when do I get to see these sketches?" he asked and smiled, as he tried to look at her notebook.

"Oh, no, you don't. Not till I'm done, but I'm making good progress so probably tomorrow. Sound good?"

"That's better than good. Thanks again, Judy."

Michael walked up the stairs to the bedroom and found Jonah hard at work at his computer.

"Hey, you're here! I have so much to show you!" Jonah launched into a long-winded explanation about why he selected Wordpress over Drupal to create the site. He also got the color scheme ideas from Judy but he said that all the branding was a placeholder for the time being. Michael could see Jonah had already put quite a bit of work into the project.

"So, yeah, if you can get me a list of all the products we carry, I'm going to make a product database for the products page. Oh, and we can even like, hook it up to an inventory system. Or maybe not. But like, I can create one. I have all these ideas that could be really cool. I think I can have this all done by the end of next week for sure!"

Michael loved how excited Jonah was about this, and Judy, too. Maybe if their dad involved Michael more in the market's decisions when he was a kid, he would have been more into it, too. Michael was even getting excited about it now. They could really turn things around. He told Jonah as much and then headed downstairs to set the table and get everything ready for dinner. His mother had called and let him know that Annie would be joining them and that they would be there shortly.

While Michael waited, he wandered into the den and thought about what Judy had said. It just might make the perfect bedroom for Mom and Dad when Dad came home. He was already walking but it would probably make things easier for him not to have to go up and down the stairs. Michael made a mental note to discuss this with his mother, when he heard voices out in the kitchen.

"Michael, Michael! Where are you?" His mother shouted enthusiastically.

He came back into the kitchen and was engulfed by her arms and her spirit.

"Michael, the outside of the house looks amazing, I can't believe what you've done!"

"Judy and Jonah helped, too, with everything," he said, indicating that all of the interior had now been painted as well.

A few seconds later, both Judy and Jonah came in and they all sat down to a lively meal. As they ate, they discussed all their ideas and plans and what they had all worked on that day, both for the Market and for their home.

As they were finishing up their pizza, Michael cleared his throat and said, "I have something to tell everyone." The room grew quiet.

"Today I went to the hospital and spoke with Dad. It was really great. He's having some trouble talking but he let me know he wants our help in coming up with ways to save the market and he wants to see us all every day, if possible." He paused. "And he and I have ... forgiven each other."

Annie let out something that sounded like a war whoop—or was it more like a whoopee—and then said, "Hallelujah, finally. That's great bro! So, what are we going to do about the market in terms of decisions?"

Michael let her know his idea of having their father actively participate in the decision-making, but no longer having it be a dictatorship market ... it would be a family market, where everyone's input counted. And that meant that Michael wouldn't be leading the charge on his own, either. Michael always believed that you needed to involve the whole team, from the mailroom people to the top executives, to come up with fresh ideas. Everyone had something to contribute.

His mother beamed.

They finished up dinner and then Michael and Annie did the dishes. Michael thought to himself that next time he ordered pizza, he needed to remember paper plates and cups.

"Sooo, thanks for babysitting the other night! Tom and I had the best time and the boys couldn't stop raving about you. They want you to come over again soon!"

Michael chuckled. "That's just because I'm a pushover and mistakenly gave the boys soda after hours."

"What? Well that must explain it." Annie winked at him.

"No, seriously. Michael, it's nice to have you back here. I feel like I have support now. For a lot of the past decade or so, it's seemed that I've been going at it alone with them. It's nice to have your help now. I mean, I'm not saying that you weren't helpful before ... well, I guess I am, but it's not like it was your fault." Annie continued to ramble. She tended to do that. It's a good thing she married such a quiet guy like Tom, Michael thought. They were well suited for each other, he decided.

"So, anyway what I was trying to say was that last night was great. Tom and I went to the Warren Inn but ate in the dining room for once. It is so nice there! So well done and the food was incredible! I feel like Beth should totally have a show on the food network!"

Annie continued for a few minutes about how the Food Network was amazing and how they should do a show based in Maine, and wouldn't it be amazing if Malone's Market could be featured? Now, there was an idea. By the time they made it back to drying the dishes, the conversation circled back to Beth. Annie wanted to know what the status was with her and Michael. Michael wanted to laugh at his sister's roundabout way of speaking, but he thought it was endearing and part of her charm, despite how frustrating it could be. He spaced out for a moment.

"So? So? You never gave me all the details about the other night. And frankly, I don't need every detail but are you going to see her again? How do you feel about her? How does she feel about you?"

This was like twenty questions, thought Michael, "Yes, I like her. And I'm unsure."

"Seriously? That's how you're going to answer

141

that question. Pish. You're just like you were when we were kids."

Michael laughed at that. They finished up the dishes and had a few more laughs before Annie headed home and the rest of the family retired to the living room, where they watched a favorite movie of Michael's, "Back to the Future." It took place in 1985, and this mad scientist type, Doc Brown, invents time travel. A young Marty McFly, played by Michael J. Fox, travels back to 1955, and accidentally prevents his parents from meeting, putting his own existence at stake. Judy had never seen it but she ended up loving it! They had a good laugh and as Michael looked around the room at his Mother, Jonah, and Judy, he realized that he couldn't think of anywhere else he'd rather be that night.

***

The next morning, Michael got up early and went for another run to the Gray Harbor Lighthouse. He secretly hoped he'd run into Beth, but she wasn't there. It was probably still breakfast service at the Warren Inn. Or maybe she didn't exercise every day. He was looking forward to their 'business lunch' tomorrow and had settled on doing a picnic in the back of Malone's. Of course he was going to be doing a little work there today in preparation for tomorrow, but also to help better the market itself. He was going to get some picnic tables and benches, wood chips, and plants. As far as Beth and thoughts of her went, he guessed it was best he didn't see her today, since there was a lot to be done aside from his picnic preparations. He wanted to talk to his mother about preparing the house for his father's return. He also wanted to work with Judy and Jonah on the website and re-branding ideas. He also needed some time to think about his own future. Huh, he thought. He kept coming back to that. His future.

He didn't know what he wanted, but he did know what he didn't want. He didn't want to be a part of Goldfarb anymore. It was time to move on. He had been there since business school and he also didn't appreciate their recent behavior towards him. He was still managing director, he thought. Maybe he needed to do something drastic. He would call his lawyer later in the day and try to set up a call and get his resignation process started.

After spending a few minutes staring out at the water, he ran back home. As he ran, he thought about all that had happened over the past week. He couldn't believe that's all the time that had passed. It seemed like so much longer. When he got home, he ran right up the stairs to the room he and Jonah were sharing and was surprised to see Jonah up already.

"Jonah, what are you doing up so early?" Michael checked his watch. "It's only seven. I'm impressed ... BUT what are you doing?"

"Building the website, you dope. Pull up a chair."

Michael did exactly that.

Jonah sniffed and said, "Oh, my God! You smell foul. All right, just stay about a foot away from me and try not to drip any of your sweat on my computer, okay?"

Michael was tempted to put Jonah in a headlock but decided against. Instead, he maturely stuck out his tongue and said, "All right little brother, I'll try not to drip on your precious computer, just show me what you have."

For the next hour, Jonah showed him how he had set up a simple database where they could load their product data so people could see what the store had to offer and even do searches. For example, what gluten-free products did Malone's Market have to offer? What kinds of fish? And the best part was he had written a script where they could just upload a spreadsheet (a properly formatted one) and it would load the data. Michael was impressed.

"Oh, and Judy is also writing all the copy, she should have it all done tonight. So basically if Dad likes this, we can launch with this and our current logo now and then relaunch with updated branding in a couple of weeks or whenever."

"I'm really impressed, Jonah," Michael said and put his arm around his little brother. You really are a brain. And you just totally freed up my afternoon. How much more work do you have to do on this?"

"Nothing, really, without that inventory list and Judy's copy — wait, why?" He regretted saying he was free very quickly.

"Perfect. Get dressed and we're going back to McAllister's. We have some work to do, and then we'll go visit Dad."

"Arrghhh. Fine, but what's in this for me?"

"I'll get you a couple of egg n' cheese rolls at the diner this morning. We'll bring Judy, too. What do you think?"

"All right, you know me, I'm a sucker for food, I'll go get Judy ... and you may want to take a shower. You really stink!"

Michael laughed at that, but it was true. He did

really stink. Running six miles never left him smelling great, but he felt good. He hopped in the shower and opted not to shave again, he was kind of liking the mountain man look but maybe he would shave it off tomorrow and reserve the look for the winter. He pulled on what had become his uniform in Maine: a pair of jeans, a t-shirt, and his boat shoes. Then he ran down stairs to an eager Judy and Jonah.

"Let's go, we're starving, Michael," said Judy. Not something he expected from his usually quiet and reserved sister. He guessed she was getting comfortable with him and that made him smile.

They walked out to the car and Michael drove them to the local diner. They ended up ordering pancakes, egg and cheese rolls, bacon, and potatoes and sharing all of it. Michael couldn't remember having such a pleasant meal ever before. They joked around, talking about music, movies, and even more serious topics like their dad and the store.

"Judy, I've been meaning to ask you. I don't know if this is your sort of thing." Michael paused and Jonah gave him a warning glance, "But I was thinking it might be really cool to have a mural in the back of the store, outside? You know by the parking lot? We're going to pick up some picnic tables and stuff for that area today so that people can sit out there and enjoy lunch. Anyway, I'm not much of an artist. And given that I know you're artistically inclined ..." Before Michael could continue, Judy paused and looked at Michael and then Jonah.

Michael realized then that maybe he shouldn't have said anything, so he tried to save himself and Jonah by saying, "You know, since you're working on the logo ... I was if wondering if you would help me with it?"

"Ouch!" Jonah shrieked, after Judy punched him hard in the arm.

"That's for telling him." Judy turned her attention back to Michael and said, "Sure, I'd love to help."

They all laughed after that and headed over to McAllister's.

After about two hours they had everything that they needed, including four picnic tables and benches, in an unfinished wood that matched the building exterior. They also purchased paint and supplies for a mural, wood chips, geraniums, potting soil, shovels, and a watering can. They scheduled for the picnic tables to be delivered in the afternoon, but packed up the rest of the supplies in Michael's car.

Judy proved to be a master gardener. By two thirty, they had all of the flowers planted and wood chips in place. They had even begun to add the base coat of paint for the mural on the wall. An hour later it was a nice beige color. Judy decided it would be best if she spent some time thinking about what to put up on the mural before starting. But even without the mural, they all decided it looked a lot better out there. The picnic tables were scheduled to arrive in thirty minutes, so they decided to hang out at the market, get a bite to eat, and visit Mom and Annie.

Judy walked in and headed straight for the cheese counter where their mother was. "Hey, Mom! How's business today?"

"Good, good. It's picked up a little. With more barbeques coming up, everyone has stopped by to buy cheese for cheeseburgers today. Unfortunately, no one

has been too adventurous today. Mostly cheddar."
Marty frowned. "So what are you kids up to today?"

Michael answered for the group, "We're working
on the picnic area project and then we're going to the
hospital to visit Dad. Are you going to head there
tonight?"

Ahh, I went this morning at eight. They have
special hours for spouses from eight to eleven. Thank
God! That's usually the slower part of the day. But I
may stop in just before eight to say a quick goodnight.
Are you kids taking care of dinner tonight?" Marty
looked hopeful.

"I'm going out with friends tonight," said Jonah.

Judy looked at Michael for confirmation and then
turned to their mother. "Michael and I will be home
tonight, Mom. We'll put something together, any
request?'

Marty looked thoughtful. "No cheeseburgers!"

Michael, Judy, and Jonah walked through the
aisles and grabbed some cheese, salami, mustard,
pickles, bread, chips, and sodas and then headed for the
register. Michael insisted on paying for it all. They then
headed out and sat on the ground and made quick
work at making sandwiches — and devouring them just
as quickly. A short time later, the delivery truck arrived
and they worked with the driver to get the tables set up.
It was starting to look really good out there. Then they
sat down and finished up their lunches and hung out,
chatting for a bit.

Michael and Judy decided on a simple dinner of
pasta, salad, and garlic bread and went back in to make
their purchases, then headed over to the hospital to
visit their father. Michael had to admit that James

seemed to have visibly improved since the day before. He still couldn't really move one side of his face or his arm but he had demonstrated his walking abilities and excitedly spoke about coming home, and coming back to the market, as soon as possible

The kids told him about the picnic area and the website. He seemed to respond well to both projects and he loved the idea of the mural. He said they had to have blueberries, the Maine tartan, lobsters, and of course a moose, integrated into the mural somehow. Everyone felt energized after seeing Dad and by five-thirty they were all home and unwinding.

Michael had a great time preparing the meal with Judy and while they worked, she confided that she wanted to go to the Rhode Island School of Design to study graphic and classical arts. She told him all about the portfolio preparation process and excitedly said that having a real company use her logo, even if it was just the family business, could really help her application.

After he, Judy, and his mother had dinner later that night, they all parted ways to do their own thing. Michael went up to his room and picked up the *Wall Street Journal* but quickly decided against opening it ... why ruin the rest of the evening? He had much more exciting things to think about, like tomorrow, and his 'business lunch' with Beth.

CHAPTER TWELVE

The next morning, Michael awoke with feelings of nervous energy. He wanted everything to be perfect. He got up and showered and shaved. He donned a fresh purple polo shirt, brown belt, jeans, wayfarer sunglasses, and his boat shoes. He looked casual but clean-cut. The night before he had managed to find a wicker basket downstairs in the kitchen and even an appropriate checkered tablecloth and napkins. He got all his utensils and cups together and then headed off to the market to get supplies and make lunch for Beth and himself. They'd be dining in the brand-new picnic area at the market that day.

At the market, he found all of the necessary ingredients to make what he hoped would be a memorable lunch. He went to the storage room and prepared classic lobster rolls a la Mama Malone, along with a string bean salad made with red potato, onions, olive oil and oregano. He also had selected various cheeses, crackers, and grapes to go with the meal, as well as some San Pellegrino. After he was done, he packed everything in the car, and headed to the Warren Inn to pick up Beth.

***

She couldn't believe the bicycle tour was finally over, thank God. Hosting the touring company was a great business opportunity, but she was also dead tired because of it. All she wanted to do was sleep. But she couldn't sleep; she was too excited about seeing Michael later. She didn't know where he was taking her, but she was pretty sure it was actually a date and that the business lunch was just pretense. Or at least she hoped it was. She remembered their brief kiss yesterday and smiled; yeah, this was definitely no business lunch. It was strange to think she had seen Michael almost every day the entire week. Bumping into him in town, at the Inn, and even on her run. Maybe it was kismet. Maybe they were meant to meet up again now at this time in their lives. Whoa, she thought to herself. Let's not get too far ahead of ourselves here. They had shared two kisses...okay, one intense kiss that lasted several hours and then a casual one.

She finished her shower and then got dressed with care, selecting a sexy red thong and matching bra. Just in case. She put on some skinny jeans and then a belted silk navy t-shirt and strappy sandals. She carefully applied light makeup and then looked at her reflection to admire the finished product. She was usually a pretty modest person, but even she had to admit she had a glow about her that day. Her hair looked great and her outfit was nice but not too nice. It was just right for dining anywhere, really.

She packed her handbag up with all she'd need for

the day and then left her cottage to head towards the Inn. By the time she arrived, she saw Michael already waiting outside, leaning up against his car. He had not seen her yet so she enjoyed this moment of observing him undetected. As she looked him over, she admired the manliness he exuded. With his arms crossed she could see the muscles in his deeply tanned arms. He looked less like a Wall Street guy today, and more like a guy who got his muscles from a hard day of work outdoors. She noticed he had shaved and that the clean-cut look worked for him as well as the more rough and tumble look he had been sporting the past few days. After a few more moments, she decided to make her presence known.

She walked towards Michael and waved to get his attention. He flashed a lopsided grin that was both sexy and genuine all at once. It lit up his whole face. She bit her lip, trying to hold back from saying something she shouldn't.

"Hi Beth! You look great," he said, as he smiled appreciatively and went around to open the car door for her. After she stepped in, he gently closed the door and walked back around to the driver seat. As he was starting the car, he looked at her and said, "Ready for our date — I mean 'business lunch.'" He smiled at her again, this time more sheepishly.

"Why, Mr. Malone, I'd like to remind you this is strictly business, " Beth attempted to say in her most professional voice.

He smiled at her and they drove in silence for a few moments, before Beth asked, "So, where exactly are we going?"

"You'll see," he said cheerfully. They pulled into

Malone's Market parking lot shortly after that.

"So here we are ... at the market?"

"Yes, I know, probably not what you're thinking, but you'll see." He exited the car and went around to help her out and then went to the trunk and pulled out what looked like a fully-stocked picnic basket.

Now this seemed more like it. She loved picnics, one thing she could appreciate about Michael is he certainly made an effort to do something she would like. She was excited to find out what lunch was!

They walked around to the side of the market, to a picnic area that she was sure was new. It was cute. There were natural wood picnic tables and benches, nice planters with beautiful flowers, and the beginnings of a mural. It would make for a really pleasant lunch spot, especially on such a beautiful day. He led her to a table and began to unpack the basket.

"So, what would you like to talk about, on our 'business lunch' Michael?" She couldn't help gesturing with quote marks to tease him.

"Okay, I cannot tell a lie. Although I do value your opinion as a business owner here in Gray Harbor ... I invited you to lunch today under false pretenses. I'd rather just learn more about you, and get to know you. BUT I also wouldn't mind hearing your opinion on what it takes to be successful in Gray Harbor ... with you ... I mean, business." He smiled sheepishly as he stole a grape from the basket and popped it into his mouth.

"Michael, I just don't know if I can stay here under these false pretenses. I'm not sure there's anything you can do to convince me otherwise ..." She gave him a devilish grin and pretended to get up.

He placed his hands on hers and said, "Well, what if I tell you what I made today, could that maybe convince you to stay?"

"Perhaps."

He smiled as he unloaded the grapes, cheese, honey for the cheese, white wine, and then finally two packages wrapped in wax paper. He handed her one and then opened and poured some wine for them.

They clinked their wine glasses and sipped. She was charmed by his efforts.

"What's this?" she asked setting down her wine glass and opening the white package.

"It's a lobster roll, but you'll see it's not exactly your traditional roll. It has its own special twist."

Beth loved a lobster roll just as much as the next person. She bit into it and her eyes opened wide. This roll was different — it was served on a top-split brioche and the lobster was served true-Maine style. Beth could taste some light mayonnaise, lemon, salt, and green pepper. It was perfectly done. She usually opted for the simple butter-only recipe, but she had to admit this was quite good. She took another bite and moaned in appreciation.

"Michael, this is delicious! Did you make this?"

Michael grinned from ear to ear. "Why, yes, I did make it, and coming from you I'll take that as a huge compliment. I do promise though …" he paused for effect, " … not to let it go to my head."

They ate in silence for a few moments and just enjoyed being outside.

"This is really nice, just being out here on a nice day, enjoying the food. There really aren't many places to go in town if you just want a casual meal. And even the Tavern isn't open for lunch."

"Yeah, I was thinking that just now, too. Not to get all 'businessy' but now that you mention it, I had put the picnic tables here so people who buy snacks can enjoy them before they hit the road again, but you may be onto something. But how would I go about serving food here at the market?"

Beth smiled and looked like she was thinking this through as she bit into her lobster roll. She explained the different approaches. Prepared foods versus made-to-order. She explained the health code restrictions for each and the pros and cons. She explained the permits, the types of refrigeration cases they should purchase. She felt like she was rambling and being boring, but Michael was taking it all in and really paying attention.

Before she knew it they had finished all of the food. They sat there and chatted a bit more about riding bicycles and where to get bikes for her business, then they both started to clean up the remnants of their lunch.

"So, I know I just said we would have lunch, but I also had something else in mind," Michael said. "Wait here and I'll be right back."

He left with the basket in hand and headed back towards the parking lot. She heard the car door slam in the distance and then listened for Michael to return. She was feeling impatient and curious when Michael came back wheeling two old cruiser bicycles. One even had a banana seat.

"Oh, my God, Michael, where did you get those ridiculous bicycles?" Beth covered her mouth and laughed out loud.

"You mean these nineteen eighties classics?" he

responded. "From my parent's garage. It's hard to get bicycle rentals in this neighborhood on short notice. But what could be more fun than watching a grown man ride around on a banana-seat bicycle for the rest of the afternoon?" He looked at her and laughed a little, and she literally felt her knees get weak.

"Don't you laugh at me, Michael. I can ride a banana seat bicycle with the best of them, so I call that one. Where are we headed?" she asked.

"Oh, you know, around," he said, smiling again.

She noticed that there was a small backpack in one of the bicycle baskets. She was intrigued.

"All right Malone, we'll do it your way," she said, as she placed her purse in the empty basket. "Lead the way!"

They rode around for hours, laughing and talking all along the way. They rode to the lighthouse and parked their bikes outside and got the tour so they could look at the view from the top. As they were standing there, Michael said, "Gosh I hope no one steals our bikes ..."

"That would be a shame, then I'd be stuck walking back with you," she said, her eyes darkening.

He stepped closer to her, his body pressing against hers. She sucked in her breath; they were pressed against each other and he was looking into her eyes searchingly. She inched closer, and so did he. Just before he was about to kiss her, she heard a voice from behind.

"Eh, hem. This is a family place," one of the lighthouse tour volunteers croaked at them. He was a salty-looking old man who probably spent most of his life out on the water as opposed to inside a lighthouse.

"We're closing up in just a few, so you best be going elsewhere." He looked at them with a spark in his eyes before he added, "My wife and I used to come here back in my day. A long time ago." He shuffled away and made his way to the steps.

Michael was trying to hide his excitement. Beth really got to him. But maybe it was best they were interrupted? He let out a breath and said, "So, maybe it's time to take this adventure back on the road?"

Beth nodded in agreement and they headed down the stairs and back to their bikes. Then they rode into town and got ice cream, walking their bicycles around. They stopped by a wine shop and bought a bottle of white wine for later that night. She hadn't planned on a marathon date but that's what the day appeared to be turning into. At around six they decided to go to Nick's pizza and get a slice.

"So, Michael," she said. "I still don't know exactly what you do for a living?"

He laughed. "Sometimes I don't know either. But in all seriousness, what I do is I help companies and people grow. Sometimes we also help them make difficult decisions. It gets complicated and sometimes it even feels a little clandestine. It can be really exciting, but I really do feel like it's time for a change for me. I've made a lot of money doing this; I've invested most of it in long term investments, but now I want out so I can invest in my own future and do something that makes me happy ... something more meaningful."

She looked pensive and then said, "Okay, so I still have no idea what that means, but it sounds like you're on to the next thing."

They discussed what that next thing could be as

they left Nick's pizza with their purchases and rode their bikes back over to the inn. It was getting chilly, but the briskness gave Beth something else to focus on besides her growing attraction to Michael. They parked their bikes in the large garage structure just behind the parking lot. It looked like an old carriage house that had been modernized a bit.

They walked out of the garage hand in hand, Michael grabbing his backpack and slinging it over his shoulder. Beth turned to Michael and said, "This was by far the best business lunch I've ever had."

He turned to her and said, "Oh, was it now?"

He came closer and she slowly dragged her hands up his arms and then linked them around his neck, looking at him. She desperately wanted to kiss him but began to doubt herself, what if it really was just a friendly business lunch? It couldn't be, she reassured herself.

Just then he lifted his head and looked searchingly into her eyes. He must have found what he was looking for because his lips pressed softly against hers. At first he gently nibbled her lips, and then he began kissing her more deeply and aggressively. She was enjoying the kiss but she began to get very warm. The truth was she wanted him to touch her. When he looked at her and kissed her with such hunger and heat, how could she think of anything else?

She slid her hands up to his shoulders as the two of them edged their way to the carriage house. Once they reached it, he dropped his bag and roughly backed her up against the wall. He pressed the hard length of his body against her, holding her hips firmly as he kissed her more deeply. He then began to kiss her throat down to her collarbone. She threw her head back in desire and tried to move his hands down her body. But he fought her and instead said, "Sometimes I like to move slowly, but first, why don't we move this inside." He picked up his bag, waiting for her to lead the way.

She led him into the dark carriage house. Once inside, his hands moved up the sides of her hips, up to her ribs, and then she slowly brushed his thumbs against the side of her breasts.

She felt like the whole world was hushed. He continued to kiss her lightly up her neck, his teeth scraping lightly over her earlobes. He slowly undid her belt buckle, which was preventing him from touching her, and threw it to the floor in one swift motion. He moved back to her mouth now and parted her lips in a deep kiss before returning his attention back to her shirt. His hands were underneath her shirt and she was in ecstasy and in hell, all at once. He pulled away and watching her face, he lifted up her shirt while still pressing against her and rolled one nipple between his fingers through the lace of her bra. She moaned with pleasure. She pressed her hips against him, indicating she wanted much, much more than just this. She needed a release from the ache inside her. She reached down and pressed her palm against the hardness just underneath his zipper. She unzipped him and slipped her hand inside.

He let out a low growl and looked at her searchingly. "Are you sure about this?"

She nodded and he moved to get something on the floor. That's right, he had a backpack. He opened it and removed a blanket, spreading it on the floor.

She arched an eyebrow and looked at him questioningly.

"I had packed this cause I thought we might do some stargazing tonight, there are some great constellations out there. But now I'm glad I have it since I'd rather look at you," he said, as he pulled her gently to the ground with him.

As they moved to the blanket, she tugged his shirt free and she skimmed her fingers over his taut stomach. He let out a gasp. He pushed her hands away and returned to kissing her neck and whispered huskily, "I just want to concentrate on you."

While kissing her, he made quick work of her jeans, unbuttoning them and pulling them off and then he removed her shirt. He paused and smiled, looking down at her red panties and bra. He reached around her and released her breasts from the fabric. He then lowered himself and sucked gently, his tongue darting across her now very hard nipples.

He thought to himself, God, Beth was sexy. She was soft, but well-toned, and her creamy, yet slightly tanned, skin perfectly complemented her masses of red hair.

He moved his hands across her thighs, then smoothed his hands over her hips and over her stomach as he looked at her intensely. His fingers then dipped underneath the elastic edges of her panties. She sucked in her breath and pushed her hips back.

She gasped. "Michael, please ..."

He touched her, his fingers seeking her heat. He slipped his fingers inside her softness and used the other hand to cup her breast. He gently bit her nipples.

The sensations built up inside her and she didn't

know if she could hold out any longer. She held onto him tightly as she began to lose control. Her body moved in a rhythmic motion against his hands, against his body. Pleasure rushed through her until she was gasping for air. She stared blindly at the ceiling as Michael held her in his arms after her orgasm. He then began to kiss her softly.

He held her there for a long time. Beth couldn't help herself, she was feeling vulnerable and raw. She had to say it. "Now what? What does this mean, Michael?" She looked at him searchingly, hoping that he would give her the answer she wanted.

Michael looked at her. He had no idea what to say, so he tried to speak what he was feeling. "What happens next," he repeated slowly, "is that we see each other again and again. And I kiss you again and again."

He began to kiss her neck, moving his way down her stomach.

"But what happens when you have to leave, Michael? To go back to New York in two weeks?"

He sighed and looked up. He was afraid of this moment. "I will have to leave, but not for good. I just need to settle things in New York before I can move forward. But Beth, this is good and I want to see more of you, I don't want this to end."

So many thoughts were going through Beth's head ... but one thing was for sure: she didn't want this night to end, either. They looked at each other with a mix of desire and questioning. Beth decided then it was time to trust herself and stop always searching for answers. She reached for him and whispered, "I want you now."

A groan escaped from Michael and he kissed her, gently at first and then more aggressively. He whispered, "You're amazing," pushing her red panties down.

She wrapped her arms around him, pressing her bare breasts against his smooth chest. She decided it was time for her to take the lead ... she kissed his chest, tasting the salt of his skin. Her hands roamed and worked their way down his body. At first she was nervous but her confidence grew as she followed the contours of his hard planes. His strong shoulders, muscled arms, the indent of his navel — and lower still.

He sucked in a breath and stopped her. "Hey, I wasn't finished," she said breathlessly.

He looked her. "Oh, we aren't finished ... but you're driving me crazy."

He took charge and turned Beth on to her back. He held her hands over her head. And teased her with his tongue starting at her ear and then he went for her neck. She wanted him badly and was lifting her hips and pressing against him seductively. He let go of her hands and worked his way down her body. He sucked each nipple slowly. She pressed his head against her and he began kissing his way down to her waist.

"Michael, you're driving me crazy, please," she said breathlessly, "I want you inside me!"

She didn't have to tell him twice. He reached for a condom in the pocket of his jeans and then unzipped his pants. He stood up and in a matter of seconds he had sheathed himself and had his arms wrapped fully around her. He gently kissed her as he moved between her legs. He flexed his hips and then pushed gently inside.

All thought was gone; for once Beth's mind was quiet and she was just in the moment, just feeling the sensations that radiated from where they were joined. She clung to him as he took her deeper and deeper. She wrapped her arms around his neck, her body rising to meet his. She teased her nipples as he surged into her.

"You have no idea what seeing you do that is doing to me," he said to her.

She looked at him half-lidded and then he plunged into her deeply. As his hands went to her back, he lifted her, changing their position so that she was now seated on top of him. She began rising and falling, sending tremors through her body.

She gasped, feeling herself tighten against him. He continued with his upward rhythmic thrusts until Beth released a guttural moan from her throat. He immediately released a moan of his own as they both collapsed onto the ground into a sweaty and satisfied heap.

CHAPTER THIRTEEN

The night had ended reasonably well considering the awkward moments Beth and Michael had after their encounter in the carriage house. Should he refer to it as an encounter? He smiled. Whatever it was, it was amazing. As their evening came to a close, they both got up and rushed to put on their clothes and say their goodbyes. He guessed they couldn't very well sleep in the carriage house all night. But he would have.

Beth excited him on so many levels — definitely physically but also intellectually and emotionally. Something that he had never really experienced before, something he'd like to experience more of.

***

That morning, he went to the hospital early with his mother to visit his father. They sat with him for a long while and told him all of the happenings at the store. Michael even showed him the draft of the new website. James seemed very pleased. They spoke with Dr. Williams, who let them know that in another week

James could come home, but that they should ready the home for him. Perhaps have him sleep downstairs, because even though he could walk, he would be challenged so many other ways each day that making something easier would be best for them all.

After they left the hospital, Michael decided to take care of things on the home front and take a break from the market for the day. He called Bob and discussed having a few guys come over and move his parents' bedroom to the den. Michael also wanted to redecorate. Bob agreed to come over in a few days and get it sorted out. Next, Michael made a call he was dreading, but it had to be done. His life needed to be put in order. At ten he got a call from his lawyer and decided to actually answer it.

"Duffy! Hey, how are you?" Michael asked. His lawyer was Peter Duffy, a great contracts attorney with lots of experience in employment law, and probably one of Michael's closest friends in New York.

"Michael! After reading the paper this weekend, I thought I'd hear from you, considering what was said about Krol Industries."

Krol was one of Michael's accounts that the twenty-five-year-old weasel was also working on.

Duffy continued. "You didn't see it did you? An announcement went out in the *Journal* this weekend. It got leaked to the press that Goldfarb wants the company sold, and Harry replaced."

Michael was stunned, Harry was Krol's CEO, and a friend.

"I need to call Harry and I need to go to Goldfarb now…" Before Michael could think, words poured out of him in a rush. "Duffy … I want to quit. And I think

I'm going to do it tomorrow morning."

"Whoa, Michael, are you sure about this?" said Duffy, his jovial tone gone now.

"I am. I really am, Duff. I just need to get a flight and close up a few things here. Can you get started on my severance negotiation paperwork and meet with me tomorrow morning?"

"You got it, meet me at seven for breakfast. We can go to Pershing at 42nd Street."

After their call ended, Michael spent the next hour making travel arrangements so he could be back in New York tonight. He was hoping to see Beth tonight, but this was important. His career and his reputation were at stake. He knew she would understand.

After arrangements had been made, he dusted off his computer and ran the numbers for Krol. It didn't look good to him, it seemed like a 'fire sale.' People would lose their jobs, and all because Goldfarb and some twenty-five-year-old kid were in a profit-taking mood.

Michael called Harry, the CEO of Krol, on his cellphone. Harry answered on the first ring.

"Michael, where the hell have you been?" said Harry in a rush of words.

"Harry, my father had a stroke, I've been out on vacation for over a week."

Michael paused, waiting for Harry to say more, and then he said, "Jeffrey Stevens has been working on my accounts and, judging from what I heard this morning, he's done a number on this one."

"Harry, I hate to say it, but I ran the numbers and I see why they're doing it. But they're missing some key information. I really think all the plans you have can really turn things around and give shareholders value. I will fly back and go talk to them tomorrow. But if this goes through ... well, I'm sorry to say, Harry, that I don't agree with it and I can't be a part of this kind of thing anymore."

"Michael, I'm not sure what to do now with all of this, but if I were you, I wouldn't want to be associated with Goldfarb. I'm not going down without a fight, I'm not ready to dust off the old resume yet. I got to go but we'll be talking."

With that, Harry abruptly hung up, but Michael knew as Harry put it, that they'd be talking. Michael, however, was going to be doing a different kind of talking to Goldfarb. This was ridiculous and highly unprofessional. Sure, the stock price could go up — but the media attention could also hurt them. And Goldfarb was usually very careful about these kinds of things. This was the first time something like this had leaked to the press. He needed to do damage control and he needed to leave right away to make it down to Portland in time to turn in his car and make his flight.

One hour later, Michael was saying his goodbyes to his family and everyone at Malone's Market. He had pulled his mother and Annie aside and explained the situation.

"I can't believe it, Michael. These people are ridiculous. You are right to quit. And poor Harry," said Annie. She continued to ramble but Michael didn't pick it all up. He waved his goodbyes and told them he'd be back soon. He had to deal with this first.

He got in his car and gunned it all the way to Portland. He was ready to move on with his life. He was ready to do the right thing.

Beth woke up a little late that morning. Lisa covered Monday breakfasts, which tended to be lighter than the weekend rush, so Beth didn't feel bad about sleeping in. She had had a great time with Michael the day before. The whole day had just been so romantic. The picnic, the bike ride, the impromptu dinner. And what happened in the carriage house was better than any stargazing she had ever done. Sure, the end of the evening was a little rushed but she thought that she and Michael could make it be more than a fling. Except she wasn't sure what her next move should be. Maybe she could cook him dinner and they could have a private night here at the Inn. She smiled at the thought as she got ready to face the day.

Mondays were generally slow at the Inn so she'd be prepping for the evening's dinner service alone for both the dining room and the Tavern. As she was chopping onions she thought it was hard to believe that she had only met—or rather, became reacquainted— with Michael that night in the Tavern just one week ago. She really wanted to call him, but knew that he had work of his own to do today, Anyway, they would see each other at the market tomorrow when she did her weekly shopping.

Today, she was going to do some things she hadn't done in awhile: she'd go for a run, she'd read, maybe even experiment on some new recipes before her shift started. It was going to be a great day, she could feel it, she thought to herself as she smiled.

Michael landed in New York at about five thirty. Before he had even made it off the tarmac, he called a real estate agent about listing his apartment for rent for now, and eventually for sale. He also called a moving company about picking up his things Tuesday afternoon, and found a storage place in Gray Harbor that he could use until he found his own place. He was stressed out about the next day and knew he had to keep himself busy. He reminded himself that this was the right thing to do. As he waited in the cab line at John F. Kennedy airport, he thought about the night before with Beth. She was so sexy. Just thinking about her made him picture the night before. Okay, he thought to himself, perhaps the airport is not the right place to think about this.

A few minutes later on his way home, he had put all thoughts of Beth out of his mind and focused on the tasks at hand. He had made some decisions about his future this past week and on the plane ride. He needed to get out while he could. Out of Goldfarb. Out of finance. And out of New York. Now, what he was getting himself into, he wasn't exactly sure. But he knew one thing for sure. It would be an adventure.

***

Beth looked at the clock on her cellphone, frustrated. Okay, she knew she'd see him tomorrow, but why hadn't he called? It was already nine and things were slowing down at the Warren, allowing Beth too much time to think things through. Maybe she should have held back the night before? Maybe she should have told him to call her today so they could make plans? Maybe — maybe she should have handled everything differently. She was second-guessing herself and that wasn't good. She knew she had had a good time and Michael had certainly gone through a lot of trouble planning yesterday. That's not something any man would do just to sleep with you. If he did, that would be completely twisted, and that wasn't Michael. He might not call today, but maybe he was just playing it cool. She smiled and relaxed, shaking her head. I'm being ridiculous, she thought to herself. And besides, she was going to see him tomorrow. Tonight she just needed to focus on getting things cleaned and prepped for the next day and make her shopping list.

***

When Michael had arrived at his apartment, the first thing he did was order Chinese food. The next thing he did was take a good look around. Packing wouldn't be too difficult. Michael went for the minimalist approach in his apartment. It was a tidy studio with a small kitchen. He never cooked so he only had the bare necessities, all of which could probably fit in one box. To his left, his bathroom was much of the same thing; nothing really to pack in there except for his shampoo, shaving cream, razors, toothpaste, and his toothbrush. The living room/bedroom was also fairly simple. He had a bed from West Elm that was dark brown and quite low to the ground. Beside it was a small stool that doubled as a nightstand and held an alarm clock and a lamp. In front of the window and in the corner stood the most expensive items in the whole apartment: his Eames Lounge chair and ottoman. They faced a small media console, which had a thirty-two-inch flat screen TV. He looked around and realized that in the four years he had lived in this apartment, he had barely put any personal touches around; he literally just ate and slept here. Well, and he ate takeout here, too.

Now was as good a time as any to start packing up what he could in terms of his clothes and other personal items. The movers would take care of the rest on Wednesday morning. His Chinese food came and he ate and then planned his attack. By the time he went to bed that evening, everything was packed except for one suit, shirt, tie, and pair of shoes he left out to wear the next day. It was amazing that he could pack up his entire home, his entire life, in just one evening.

***

That next morning, Michael was up at the crack of dawn to meet with Duffy. He took a cab over to Pershing Square to make it to the seven o'clock meeting on time. Duffy was already there, drinking coffee.

"Hey, Michael! How you doing this morning?" Duffy asked, grinning.

Michael shook his head. Duffy had to be the most cheerful lawyer in Manhattan. It frustrated Michael sometimes, but it also was one of his favorite things about the man. Michael sat down and nodded good morning. Duffy waved over the server to bring him more coffee, and a cup for Michael.

"So, find anything for me in the documents?" Michael asked.

"Well, no severance, of course. The agreement is pretty ironclad if you quit. The good news and bad news is that your contract was up three months ago. You know the one they delayed resigning? So we can't get the rest of your promised income, which would barely be worth the fight since it's based on profits. The thing that's really great, though, is your stake in the company. "

"I think I'm at five percent now. What does that have to do with anything?" Michael asked, confused.

"That means they owe you five percent of the holdings ... in cash. The better part is they have it, and don't even know it yet. Check it out." Duffy pulled out a copy of the paper and passed it over to Michael. Goldfarb announced a new partner who was going to be putting in cash ... which meant Michael's five percent just got a lot larger ... that meant Michael could walk away with eighty million dollars.

He was stunned. When he came to the fund five years back, they were a small, two million dollar shop. He must have done something right for them to now be worth several hundred million dollars. He was absolutely floored.

"Wow. How is that going to affect them when I pull out a stake like this?"

"They should have thought about that before all of this. I got us a meeting at nine with your whole team. They think it's a contract negotiation though ... that's how I got the meeting. And I don't think they're expecting you to be with me, as they let me know you're on vacation. But I think that is a good thing, don't you?"

Michael smiled. He knew that no one at Goldfarb, especially management, liked surprises. Especially a surprise that meant them losing money, along with the threat of more negative press including the fact that Michael was leaving, in part, due to their mishandling the Krol situation and to Goldfarb uncaringly deciding the fate of thousands of people. That kind of news always left a bad taste in people's mouths and would really hurt business.

Three hours later, Michael and Duffy were sitting before the board, negotiating the terms of separation. The board members were certainly not pleased with Michael, but they were also displeased with the bad press that had been leaked out to the media about their dealings with Krol. During all of it, Michael couldn't stop thinking about Beth. Before Beth, he had only dated self-interested women who really didn't care about him. He knew things with Beth were new ... but he also knew they had something. Something special. He couldn't wait to get back to Maine and back to Beth.

***

It was Tuesday and Beth was having a bad day. She had received a call from Bob with gossip, as usual. He had heard something about how Michael was gone already. That he had a flight the day before to NY. Michael's mother had told Bob that, as usual, Michael couldn't get the NY bug out of him and he took off immediately. Beth couldn't understand it. How could he just sleep with her and then take off like that without a word to her. Was it all just some game to him?

She decided Bob had to be wrong and wanted to find out for herself exactly what was going on. She took extra care with her appearance after the breakfast rush and got to the market a little later than usual. She couldn't find Michael anywhere. She finally tracked down Annie so she could do her shopping.

"Hey, Beth! How are you today? Did you see the new picnic area that Michael set up? You'll have to check it out. So, I was watching the Food Network the other day and you're just going to love this. We have scallops pretty regularly so I thought of this for you. Giada made prosciutto wrapped scallops. Does that just sound to die for?" Finally, Annie paused.

"Are you okay, Beth?"

"Um, oh, you know, just a busy day at the Inn. Hey, you haven't seen Michael around today, have you? We were going to discuss some ideas he had for the Inn this week, but I haven't heard from him." Beth tried to play it casual, which seemed to work on Annie.

"Oh, yeah. He had to take off back to New York in a hurry yesterday. I am not entirely clear on what happened with him. But he was a wreck yesterday morning. I just know he'll be back soon. And when it comes to business and things, Michael always keeps his word, so I'm sure you guys can discuss things soon," Annie said in a distracted tone.

When it came to business, sure, but what about with relationships? Did they even have a relationship? What exactly was going on here, Beth wondered.

"Oh, hey, Beth, here are those fresh blueberries for the blueberry pancakes recipe. Man, those just can't get enough of them, huh?"

Beth couldn't focus on blueberries now. She began to wonder if she had done something wrong. Maybe she was too forward with Michael?

"Hey, Beth? You still there?" Annie looked at her with concern.

"Oh, yeah. I'm fine, just lost in thought, I guess."

"Oh, don't we all get that way sometimes," Annie said, giving her an understanding look as she steered Beth through the store.

Annie continued to ramble for the next hour while she helped Beth with her order.

Beth couldn't focus. She couldn't believe he left without so much as a phone call after the day and night they shared. She was wrong about him; he wasn't one of the good ones. Now all she could think about was how she wished she had never let Michael get to her. She thought they shared something special but now, she was starting to see it for what it was ... just moments of fleeting passion. Nothing more. She sighed and tried to hold back the tears that were forming.

***

It was finally done and what a day it had been. He quit his job and got his stake in the company returned to him... which was now worth millions upon millions. He had his apartment packed up and showed it to a real estate agent, who would keep him posted on renting it out for the time being. Now he was exhausted. He changed out of his suit and into what had become his "Maine Uniform." He put on his jeans, polo, and boat shoes.

He sat on the floor of the now-empty apartment, save for a duffle bag, a small backpack, and a laptop computer. He looked for flights and found one leaving JFK that evening for Portland, Maine, he booked it and a rental car. With any luck, he'd be home in the late evening or very early morning. Home. There he'd said it. Maine was home, and he felt good about that.

He decided that it was time to go; he'd grab a bite

to eat at the airport. He took one last look at the apartment before closing the door. He went outside and hailed a cab. He had no idea what was next for him, but he felt like he didn't have to rush things. He was, however, excited to get back to Maine and actually implement some of the changes at Malone's Market that he and his family had been discussing. He was also excited to figure out what was next for him career wise ... and he was excited to see Beth.

CHAPTER FOURTEEN

Michael arrived in Portland in the very early hours of Wednesday morning and went to pick out a rental car. This time he went with just a standard Chevy Malibu sedan, something Jonah wouldn't be nearly as excited to drive. He put his bags in back and drove the hour and a half to Gray Harbor. He decided not to drive straight home. Instead, he bought a paper in town and went to the diner to kill a little time. He still felt like he needed some time to process things.

Michael spent the morning just relaxing and thinking about what could be next. After he finished his breakfast, he wandered through the various shops in town. He decided to visit his father and tell him the good news.

When he arrived in his father's room, he could see a cloud had settled over James Malone.

"Hey, Dad, how's it going?" Michael asked cautiously.

James struggled to speak but after several moments, said, "Tough daaya. Ti-Tired. Therapy. Fru-us-strated. Wannnt tooo goo home." James paused and looked like he was thinking about something. "Whhhyyya rrrr yoooou here? New York?" he asked, with a questioning look.

"It's a long story, Dad, but it's part of why I came here today." Michael took in a deep breath before continuing, "I resigned from my position at Goldfarb. I decided I didn't like the way they wanted to do business. I want to do something a little more meaningful than count money, you know?"

With that, James chuckled.

Michael smiled. "Well, okay, I have to admit I liked counting the money when I walked out the door yesterday, Dad. I ended up walking away with a nice chunk of change. But I've decided to come back here and start my own business and help with our family business, if the offer still stands to be a partner. I know I'm about thirteen years late, but I'd like to help now and I can contribute what you, Mom, and Annie will let me in terms of an investment."

James Malone's face went blank for a few moments, but it appeared that he was thinking. Finally, he nodded to Michael to indicate he wanted the notebook and paper from his tray. Michael handed them to his dad and James carefully wrote out a note.

Michael was all nerves. What if his father was upset by what he had said, or wanted him to have no part in all of this? After a few more minutes of James struggling to write his thoughts down, he motioned for Michael to grab the notebook and read it.

Michael looked down at the note and began reading out loud, cause some of the text was difficult to make out. "I am sorry you left your job, but it sounds like it was time. Welcome aboard!! I am happy you want to invest but I want it to be fair. Each of you children gets a share so you have to calculate what an appropriate amount to invest is and let the whole family decide. Work out the details with Annie and your mother but let me know what you come up with. I trust that things are in good hands with you and the rest of the family. So does this mean you are moving back?"

Michael paused. "Geez, Dad, that was a novel, you made me sweat!"

James Malone smiled and Michael went over and hugged him. James said," Sooo are you heeree to stayay?"

"Yes," Michael said with a grin.

James perked up and Michael told him some of his ponderings about what was next. It felt good. These were the things Michael always wanted to be able to discuss with his father but hadn't been able to for the past thirteen years. He wanted to make for lost time, not only with his father but also with the whole family. And with Beth. Beth — he had almost forgotten about her. He needed to call her tonight and tell her the good news! But first, he was off to Malone's Market.

***

Beth was not herself that day. Usually baking early in the morning really calmed her. Being in the kitchen alone creating something that would start off people's day really challenged and fulfilled her. Today she just wanted to be home so she could analyze what was happening, or rather, what wasn't happening. Michael hadn't called. She had seen him Sunday. Today was Wednesday. Even by guy standards, it was about time he called, especially after what they had shared. She was wondering what she had done wrong. The one time she opened herself up to someone, and was open ... she shook her head.

After breakfast service was over, Lisa arrived in her sous chef uniform ready to prep for the evening's service.

"Hey! How's it going, Beth! Sorry I'm late but you're going to love what I've come up with for a potential special for tonight!" She looked at Beth and it then registered that something was not quite right.

"Are you okay? You don't look so good."

Beth wasn't going to unleash the whole story on her little sister. But she gave her the details of the date Sunday, including the picnic lunch, the bike ride, the walking through town, pizza — she didn't mention the Carriage house incident. Lisa was her LITTLE sister, after all. She also told her about going to the market on Tuesday and seeing Annie, and Annie's response. Michael clearly hadn't told anyone in the family about Beth or their date — and he and Annie were close. That was clear and it was something Beth knew all along.

"Huh. That doesn't add up. He clearly likes you. And I mean Annie. Well, Annie is a rambler, so if something was wrong, she would have told you, right?"

"Yeah, I guess so."

"And I mean, it's only been like three days. At school, if a guy calls me before three days then I think he is too eager. But I mean, it sounds like he was eager, so why would he wait. I dunno, sis, why don't you call him, maybe? Or like, I can find out if he's coming back from Judy or Jonah, right? I see them at Nick's Pizza all the time on the weekends."

Beth thought about it for a moment. Maybe she was being crazy. But he had to have known that you don't do this to a woman with whom you've been intimate. But she wasn't going to reduce herself to someone who let her little sister do her bidding for her.

"No, no. You're right. I'll call him and figure it out. You know, that's what I'll do right it now."

Beth grabbed her phone and called Michael, but it went straight to voicemail. That's strange, she thought. Maybe his phone was dead, or maybe he had lost it. Of course then he wouldn't have her number. Or maybe he just didn't call? She tried to tell her brain to stop.

She spoke clearly and left a message. "Hey, Michael, it's Beth. I haven't heard from you and wanted see that everything is all right? Call me." She hung up the phone and looked to Lisa.

"How was that?"

Lisa looked skeptical and then said, "I think it was okay. I mean, it's just a voicemail message after all. I'm sure he'll call. Probably tonight," she said with a smile.

Beth calmed down. Yeah, he would probably call tonight, especially after her message. She relaxed a little and then said, "Okay, so enough about that. What have you got for me for the menu tonight?"

CHAPTER FIFTEEN

After leaving the hospital Michael went to the market to see his Mom, Annie, Jonah, and Judy with pizzas on hand.

He told them about everything that had happened in New York and he gave them the details of his visit with his father. They were thrilled! Michael thought after that he'd get to rest, but Annie put him to work right away to calculate shares and see what his investment could be so they could get bills paid, buy inventory, and get the rest of the renovations completed.

He spent the rest of the afternoon trying to value the company, doing SWOT analysis (Strengths, Weaknesses, Opportunities, and Threats) and finally came up with a number that he thought would work. The amount would allow them to add an office on the first level of the store for their father, close off the elevator shaft for time being, finish the office space upstairs, finish the basement storage area and stock it, and add a prepackaged food area and deli counter so they could feature his mother's Lobster rolls, as well as other sandwiches. That would work perfectly for attracting more tourists who were looking for a reasonably-priced lunch they could take to go, or eat right there in the new picnic area. There were a few other things he thought they could add that Judy had found in the customer feedback box, including stocking Maine newspapers and magazines and maybe even some basic souvenirs, and designating an area for local business people to post flyers on corkboards. This could make it feel more like a community ... like a family.

He felt good about this. He didn't want to work for the market full time, but he could certainly put in enough hours to manage the finances. He was going to have Duffy draw up some paperwork so they could get this settled and Michael could start writing checks for the business.

The other major occurrence of the day had been that they deciding to move forward with the plans to renovate and move his parents' bedroom to the downstairs den and they also decided to redo the dining room to make it an office/exercise room for James. It had been used as an office for years anyway. The project would take a little time but it would be the best thing for James when he came home. They still didn't know when that would be, but one thing was for sure. With all of the Goldfarb money Michael had from their parting, he was going to make sure James had the best medical care possible — and he thought his family just might let him without a fight this time around. When he offered to buy a new car, however, his mother balked.

"What? They don't make a better car than the old

wagon, I am taking that thing to the grave."

Jonah had looked hopeful until his mother said, "I see that look Jonah, and you aren't getting a car, either, especially not from your brother. A cellphone or a computer is one thing; a car is a whole 'nother!"

The evening had ended on a positive note and Michael was ecstatic. He had the day off from Malone's the next day and he was pretty happy about that.

He wanted to focus on himself that next day. He needed to figure out his living situation, work situation, and his personal life in general. His personal life ...

Oh, God, he thought. It was Thursday already and he hadn't spoken to Beth since their date Sunday and since their night ...

He grabbed his phone and noticed he had a message. When had that happened? He listened to it and became concerned. Beth sounded terrible in her message. "Hey, Michael, it's Beth. I haven't heard from you and wanted see if everything is all right. Call me."

Oh, no. He hoped he hadn't jeopardized things with her. Oh, God, it had been four days. He felt like an idiot. He hoped it wasn't too late. Beth could be a little stubborn. Michael jolted out of bed.

He ran to the bathroom and showered but skipped shaving. He dug into his duffel bag and grabbed a pair of jeans and a green t-shirt and his boat shoes and got dressed. How could he not think of her the past four days? Well, that wasn't true; he had thought of her, he thought of her in every action he took towards moving to Maine. He wasn't sure where they had been going in terms of a relationship, but he knew he wanted one. He wanted to get to know her better and see if they could work as a couple.

That's it; he was going to the Inn — okay, bad idea. It was the middle of breakfast service. He decided to go to the market to see Annie and see what she would do in his situation. He ran down the stairs quickly and was out the door in what felt like only a few moments.

When he arrived at the market, it had its usual Thursday crowd. Not terribly busy but it was consistent. When Michael went inside he found Annie right away, clipboard in hand, marking something down.

"Annie," Michael said, out of breath.

"Hey, little brother, what's up? I thought you weren't coming in today?" Annie barely looked up from her pad as she made notations.

"I wasn't but I have a problem and I needed someone to talk to. Preferably a woman, and you were the closest thing I could think of, " Michael said sarcastically. That got Annie's attention.

"Ha, ha. What's up?"

"Annie, I think I may have screwed things up with Beth ..."

"Huh, I didn't know you had things to screw up yet." She stopped looking at her clipboard and looked at Michael questioningly. "Let's go up to my office."

Michael followed her up the stairs and into her office and took a seat in one of the metal folding chairs she had in front of her desk.

"Okay, so what happened exactly?"

Michael told her about the date during the day on Sunday and gave some, but not all, of the details of their evening. He told her about the message Beth left Wednesday night and how they hadn't spoke in four days.

"Annie, you must have seen her, right? Did she mention me?"

Annie was pensive and then she had a look on her face that said, "Oh, no!"

"Annie? What do you know?"

"Well ... she came in Tuesday asking about you. And actually come to think of it, she was pretty decked out. That should have tipped me off but it didn't. I was so excited to tell Beth about a new recipe Giada had on the Food Net—"

"You and the Food Network, it's a real problem, Annie," Michael said, trying to make light of the situation.

"Okay, Okay, point taken. Anyway, she said something about a business lunch and an upcoming meeting. I told her that you had left for New York, actually kind of suddenly, and that I didn't have all the details."

Michael was a little angry. "Why would you say that?"

"I had no idea what had happened Sunday and in my defense, I didn't know what was confidential about your meeting in New York so I was playing it safe and not saying anything about the specifics of your trip. You know how hard that is."

"So, now what do I do? Do I call her? Do I show up with flowers?"

After playing through the various scenarios, they decided that flowers were an admission of guilt. Instead Michael should call ASAP and then head over. Michael thanked Annie for her advice and then walked outside to the picnic area near the parking lot to make the call.

He dialed her number and it rang and rang and then went to voicemail. Maybe she was ignoring him. He needed to make sure he didn't sound like he had done anything wrong in his message. After the beep, he said," Beth! I got your message, I just got back to Gray Harbor this morning. I have so much to tell you. It was crazy in New York. I'd love to go out, or meet up this weekend or earlier, depending on your schedule. Give me a call." He hung up. He wondered if he sounded too nonchalant. Too late now. He just hoped that they could work it out.

***

So he hadn't called her back last night. Looks like Michael was no better, and possibly even worse, than one of Lisa's culinary school boys. What had she been thinking? He just tried to sweep her off her feet before leaving, got what he wanted, and left. Well, he nearly got what he wanted. That didn't sound like Michael at all ... but people change.

After all, she always thought he'd do something more creative, not become a finance guy. And well, those guys had a reputation for being real jerks. Not that there was anything wrong with finance ... it just didn't seem to fit who she thought he was. But Beth thought, I guess I thought wrong.

Beth continued with her day. She baked early in the morning, cooked various breakfast dishes for guests, and started to clean up. Then her phone rang. It was him. What should she do? Should she answer it? Should she not answer? Before she could make up her mind, it was too late; her voicemail must have picked up. She stared at her phone and then listened to the message.

So much to tell me, she thought. You could have called! Calm down, Beth, calm down, she told herself. Well, two could play at this game. She'd wait to call him, too!

Michael decided to give it some time before he ran over to Warren inn to see Beth, to give her a chance to call him back. In the meantime, he called Duffy to get the paperwork for Malone's Market finalized and sent to his family members. He contacted the real estate agent about his potential home in Gray Harbor. No news there yet, but when he called his agent in New York, he found out she had already found a renter.

Two hours had passed. It was already noon, so Michael headed into town to get a slice of pizza. He went to Nick's Pizza and ordered two slices of pepperoni and a coke. After he ate, he stared at his phone impatiently, willing it to ring — it didn't. At one thirty he couldn't take it anymore. He got in his car and drove to the Inn. He knew it was a bad idea, but he didn't know what else to do; he had to see her.

The whole way there he rehearsed what he would say once he found her. He knew that this could work if they gave each other a chance.

He pulled up to the Inn and took a deep breath. He got out of the car and headed right for the reception area. The receptionist was an older woman, possibly Beth's grandmother? He didn't see the family resemblance so he doubted it.

"Hi, is Beth Adams available, please?"

"Sure, she's in the kitchen. Let me call and see if she's available. What's your name?"

"Michael Malone, thank you"

The receptionist called the extension and said, "Hey, I have a Michael Malone here for Beth. Can you see if she's available? Yeah, I'll hang on."

"Beth, that Michael guy is here at the reception desk," Lisa called out to her sister.

"What?"

"Yeah, aren't you psyched?"

"No, no I'm not psyched. He called a few hours ago and I haven't called back. What's he doing here? Oh, God, do you think he came here to tell me he doesn't want to see me anymore?"

"Um, er. I don't think so. But I guess either way you should talk to him. Hang on, Beth. Yeah, Mirna, I'm trying to locate Beth. Yes, yes, I know the kitchen isn't that big, just hang on." Lisa looked at her sister and when Beth failed to respond, she picked up the phone and said to Mirna, "Tell him she'll be there in a just a second. Okay, yeah, goodbye."

"What are you doing Lisa? Didn't you hear me?"

"Yeah, I heard you and you're being ridiculous. Just go talk to the man and sort it out once and for all. Oh, and I'm coming with you. I want to check him out." Lisa smiled as she nudged Beth forward towards the kitchen door. "Go on, get!"

"Okay, okay, fine." Beth composed herself, smoothed her hair, and walked out of the kitchen and through the corridor to the reception area.

When she walked out, she saw Michael leaning against the wall next to the reception desk, looking very serious.

Oh, no, she thought. He didn't want anything to do with her. It's fine, she thought to herself, you can handle this, Beth.

"Hi, Michael," Beth said in a tone she felt was professional.

Michael's whole face lit up and he went up to her. "Beth, it's so good to see you!"

Huh, that wasn't what she expected.

"Can we go somewhere to talk?" He looked hopeful.

She looked at him closely. Why was he here? He had waited four days to call her back and now all of a sudden things were so urgent?

"Sure, follow me. We can talk out back in the yard." This couldn't be good, or could it, she wondered.

She led him to the Adirondack chairs in the far corner of the yard, where they had spent that first evening together kissing in the moonlight.

After they were seated, Michael said, "Beth, I'm so sorry I didn't call, I—"

"No explanation needed, Michael, but after the day and the evening we spent together, I thought I would get a phone call at the very least to tell me you were leaving?"

"You're right. I should have called but I was under the impression that if I had to focus on my career and future for a few days, you'd be okay with it, just like I was okay with your bike tour."

Okay, so he had a point there but that was beside the point. Him saying that just served to make her angry.

He reached for her hands and she stood up abruptly, before he could say another word.

"Listen, Michael, it was nice of you to stop by and

all ... but as it does for you ... my career comes first. I have to get back to the kitchen, you can show yourself out."

Michael had chills; she was so calm and cold. But he couldn't just let her walk away from him!

"Beth, wait! One of the big reasons I'm here to stay is you!"

It was too late, he thought; she was already headed back inside to the kitchen. He had so much he wanted to tell her, but clearly that didn't matter to Beth. She didn't care what his reasons were. And after all, they weren't really in a relationship and he guessed now they wouldn't be. He kicked the Adirondack chair and stormed off to the parking lot. Now what, he thought?

CHAPTER SIXTEEN

Beth couldn't believe the nerve! He seriously thought he could just come back and pick up where they left off? What happened in New York? She guessed she would never know, cause she certainly wasn't going to speak to Michael again, she thought, as she stormed into the kitchen.

"Whoa, Whoa! What's up with you?" said Lisa with a slightly bewildered look.

"Thank God I'm not trying to cook a soufflé or something, you're stomping around like a crazed beast."

"CRAZED BEAST! Seriously? Lisa, he's ridiculous!"

"Gotcha, so he did get to you, what's up?" said Lisa, her expression much more relaxed.

"Arrghh. He tried to say that he went to New York for work, that he was understanding when I couldn't see him because of the bike tour, but I mean, how does that even compare? We hadn't even been on

191

a date yet!"

Both Lisa and Beth were silent for a moment.

"Is that all he said?" Lisa said, while looking innocent. "I mean, he didn't say anything else?"

Beth looked at her wryly. "You were eavesdropping, weren't you?"

"Well ... um, yes, yes, I was."

"Okay, fine. He also said I was a big part of the reason he decided to make a move to Maine."

"Interesting."

"Geez, Lisa, just spit it out. What are you trying to say?"

"Well, I mean it's just interesting that the guy managed to potentially quit his job and pack up his whole life in New York in four days and came to see you to tell you that after just one date with you," said Lisa, with a knowing glance.

Beth was annoyed now. Could Lisa be right? Could Michael really have packed up his life and moved back here for her? She couldn't think about it now. She had too much to do and she needed to focus on the tasks at hand. There would be plenty of time later to think things through.

***

Now what, he thought to himself again. Somehow 'now what' ended up being Michael alone at the local dive bar, drinking alone in the afternoon. He replayed the scene with Beth over again in his head as he chugged the rest of his beer. He looked at the empty bottle and thought to himself, "Why are women so frustrating!"

"Bartender!" Michael called out to the burly man

in a red plaid shirt who was minding the bar. "Can I get another beer and a scotch neat?"

"Sure thing, buddy." The bartender tipped the bill of his ball cap and then grabbed Michael a beer and poured a scotch. He set the drinks in front of Michael and then made his way to the other side of the bar. Michael stared at his drinks before picking up his scotch and starting to drink. He liked this; he was starting to feel numb. Like before Beth, he had felt this way. He'd been going through the past thirteen years of his life completely numb, like a machine. Just going through the motions of his personal life and pushing himself to the limits professionally. He tried to think back to when he became this way, as he took the last sip of his scotch and started on his beer. He guessed it had started not long after Jesse's death. He always had to remain in control of his feelings and emotions and just do what was expected. And finally, when he couldn't take that anymore, he ran away. Just like he had done with Beth.

He took another sip of his now second glass of scotch ... or was it his third? He thought to himself that he never really told Beth how he felt. He knew he felt a connection between them but it had all happened so fast.

Michael grumbled to himself as he pounded away another beer and called the bartender over. He started on his, what was it now? He had no idea how many drinks he had had at this point. But he knew he had stop. He looked at his watch. It was nearly ten. He looked around the bar, which had really filled out. He paid his tab and stumbled out of the bar, which was really no more than a ramshackle cottage with dirt parking spaces. He walked over to his car and leaned against it.

No, he wouldn't do it. He wasn't going to drive. Too much tragedy had already happened in his life and he wasn't going to get behind the wheel in his present state. He picked up his cellphone and dialed Annie's number.

"Annie! It's me, Michael," he said, slightly slurring his words.

"I went to the Inn. It was bad, now I am at the dive bar next to the ice cream shop and I can't drive." He started to feel nauseous.

He hung up; all he could hear was crackling on the other end of the line. Oh, well, he thought he'd get there on his own, or maybe Annie would call back. He put his keys in his pocket and stumbled towards home. It was several miles away but he could make it.

***

Beth looked up at the clock in the Inn's kitchen— eleven o'clock She couldn't believe it. It had felt like years since Michael had come by and they talked. She felt like an idiot. Four days wasn't really that much time, all things considered. And they had only gone out on one date technically, even though it felt like so much more. Maybe she overreacted? She had let her temper get the better of her. Was she really going to let her temper and her pride get in the way of something that could be so much more than she dreamed? Love. She was scared but in their brief time together, Beth was feeling things she hadn't ever felt before. She didn't want to give those feelings a name necessarily or say them out loud ... but she was interested in Michael and she did want to give it another chance. She just had to stop playing games and pick up the phone.

She reached for her phone but before she could begin to dial, it rang Beth jumped, startled. She saw Annie's name on the display screen and answered.

"Hello?" Beth strained to hear over some static.

"Beth! Thank God! Are you with my brother? Have you seen him today at all?"

Worry started to set in. "Well, yes I saw him early this afternoon but we ..." She was embarrassed to say it. "We ... we had an argument and I haven't seen or heard from him since."

"So he hasn't come by?"

"No."

"Great, well, he called me and he mentioned the Inn, he mentioned a bar by the ice cream shop, and then he said bye. He sounded ridiculously drunk, and his car is missing."

"Oh, God," exclaimed Beth. She couldn't lose another person she loved. Oh, God, she said it. She loved Michael, and she would not lose him to some stupid car accident. Suddenly she was in control.

"Okay, Annie. Let's calm down. There are only a few places he would go, right? Here at the Inn, your parents' house, or the market. Let's start there. I'll check the Inn and the bar he mentioned. You check the market and your parents' house. Call me if you find anything, and I'll do the same, okay?"

"Thanks, Beth, you're right. Let's stay calm. I'll get in my car now and check. I'll call you soon."

With that they hung up the phone and Beth went in search of her car keys. She hoped she could find Michael before it was too late.

Michael had hit his head and there was blood, lots of it. He felt a pain in his side. What was going on? He slowly lifted himself up. He felt like he'd been hit by a truck. He looked around at his surroundings. No truck, no anything, just him on the side of the roadway. He slowly took off his t-shirt, careful to not hurt his ribs.

"Arrgh. What the hell did I do?" He looked around now as he bunched up his t-shirt and compressed his head. From the looks of it, he had stumbled as he walked along the roadway and hit his head while tumbling over the metal rails lining the roadways. He reached around for his phone. He must have lost it in his fall. He would look for it but that seemed too hard right now.

"Focus, Michael, focus," he said to himself.

He leaned against the metal rails and with one hand, he held his shirt to his bleeding head and with the other, he hitchhiked. Well, at least he didn't drive.

***

"Anne, It's me, Beth," she said frantically.

"He's nowhere near the Inn and his car is still at the bar!"

"So he's on foot, then. Okay, not good, but better than him driving."

"So now what?" asked Beth, fear creeping into her voice.

"Okay, let's try to stay calm. I am going to drive slowly up to my parents. Do me a favor and call the hospitals, just in case?"

"Okay, but call me as soon as you find out anything," said Beth.

They hung up and Beth wandered from the bar to

the Malone home at a snail's pace in her car. She hoped
Michael was okay. She couldn't believe it, one minute
she wanted him out of her life and the next, she was
worried about living life without him. She followed the
bend in the road and came upon a car and an
ambulance on her left. She pulled her car up behind
them and quickly got out. She saw Annie standing
beside the ambulance.

"Annie," Beth shouted and waved as she ran up.

Annie saw Beth and pulled her in to a hug, she
was sobbing.

"Thank God. Thank God, he's okay. My idiot
brother, who walks in the dark after drinking like that!"

Beth breathed a sigh of relief and hugged Annie
back.

"So he's okay?"

"See for yourself, they're just loading him in."

She turned around and saw him on a gurney. Oh,
my God, she thought, did she drive him to this? No,
she wouldn't blame herself for this. She was glad he
seemed okay, and when she was sure of that, she'd give
her a piece of her mind; she had been worried sick!

"Michael! You're okay!"

He turned his head as they were loading him in
and mumbled, somewhat deliriously, "Beth ..."

Beth turned to Annie. "Annie, I'll follow him to
the hospital and make sure he's all right tonight.

"All right, that works," said Annie, as she watched
the EMTs shut the ambulance doors.

Beth gave Annie an understanding nod. "Don't
worry, Annie, I have it covered."

"I'll come to the hospital with you, he's going to
be okay, Beth. I know what you're thinking, this isn't

your fault." Annie sighed and tried to put a cheerful face. "That knucklehead in the ambulance is the one who is to blame, but let's forget that now and just go."

Twenty minutes later, Beth and Annie were at the hospital. Annie went in directly with Michael while Beth stayed in the waiting room. Three hours later, Michael was discharged. He looked awful. Annie clutched his arm and walked him out, as Michael winced with pain.

Before Beth could say a word, Annie said, "So he has a few broken ribs, stitches on his hairline, but no concussion...thank God."

She shook her head and looked at her brother. "I got to give it to you, Mikey, you never do anything half-assed. When you break something, you do good work."

He grumbled out to her and was about to say something when he saw Beth.

"Beth, I ..."

"All right, well, I'm going to get some coffee, do either of you want some ... um, okay ... I'm going now." Annie quickly walked away without another word for once.

"Michael." Beth turned to him and touched his face.

He wore a pained expression. "Beth, I can explain ..."

"Don't. There will be plenty of time to talk later, I'm just glad you're okay."

"Beth, I'm so, so sorry. I was an idiot." He looked at her pleadingly.

She smiled faintly and said, "Yes, yes you are, Mr. Malone. You are quite possibly the biggest idiot in all of Maine ... but for some reason, I'm still willing to give you a chance."

She was silent and starred down at the floor.

He reached out for her. "Beth, one of the big reasons I'm back in Maine to stay is you." He paused. "I tried to tell you earlier, but I was an idiot."

"You're here to stay?" She was softening a bit.

"Yes."

She was weary but she couldn't suppress the excitement bubbling inside her.

"All I could think about was that was I holding on to my life in New York and these people who didn't care about me when I had you and my family here in Maine."

Beth listened carefully.

"You have been the first thing I thought of in the morning and the last thing before I go to bed each night. Give me a chance to show you how right we can be for each other?"

He looked at her searchingly.

Beth looked back at Michael as he inched closer and she saw how sincere he looked.

"I'll think about it," she said. "But you're going to have to think of a way to make this up to me."

She leaned over and kissed him on the lips. They parted and Michael said, "I'll enjoy making it up to you every day for the rest of our lives."

Michael leaned over and kissed Beth. It felt like he was finally home for the first time.

ABOUT THE AUTHOR

After spending years working in the fast-paced business world, author J.J. Bryant is happy to be living her dream of writing romance. She has her MBA and you may see her bring a little of that experience into the lives of her characters. J.J. Bryant grew up in New England and loves hiking and biking with her family and her miniature schnauzer puppy.

You can find J.J on the web at:
www.jjbryantbooks.com.

COMING SOON FROM
J.J. BRYANT

Lisa Adams can't complain. Her life is finally on the right track. She just finished culinary school, she works with her sister as a sous chef at the successful Warren Inn and she has a boyfriend—kind of. But something feels like it's missing. Things would be perfect if something tall, sexy and muscular …something like Evan McAllister…would just stay out of her way. But with unexpected renovations being made to the Inn all summer and Evan in charge of the project, the late-summer heat might not be the only thing steaming up Gray Harbor this August…

Watch the sparks fly August 2015 in Book 2 in the Gray Harbor Series, *Indian Summer*

21398250R00127

Made in the USA
Middletown, DE
28 June 2015